Deader 'n a Doornail
Book 5: Crystal Creek Mysteries
M. Sue Alexander

This book is a work of fiction. Names and characters in the story are a product of the author's imagination. Any resemblance to actual persons, living or dead, events or locales, is coincidental. Should you purchase a copy of this book without a cover, be aware this book may be stolen property and neither the publisher nor the author has received payment for a "stripped book."

Book 5: Crystal Creek Mysteries
Dead 'r in a Doornail
ISBN 9798896191926
SUZANDER PUBLISHING
Copyright © 2024 by M. Sue Alexander

All rights reserved by author. No part of this book may be reproduced in any form, either by electronic or mechanical means, including information storage and retrieval systems, without obtaining written permission from the publisher, except by a reviewer who may quote brief passages in a review. Scripture quotations are from *The Living Bible*. Copyright © 1971, Tyndale House Publishers; Wheaton, Illinois 60187, and used by permission. All rights reserved.

Book Cover by Christine Roszak

View M. Sue's Amazon Author and Facebook Page

M. Sue Alexander

Series Titles by Author

Resurrection Dawn 2014 Series
Book 1: Resurrection Dawn 2014   Book 2: The Christian Fugitive
Book 3: Rebels in Paradise   Book 4: Veil of Lies
Book 5: The Anointing   Book 6: Countdown to Justice
Book 7: All Rise   Book 8: Unlikely Suspect
Book 9: Lethal Snapshot   Book 10: Purgatory
Book 11: April Fool's Day   Book 12: Reign of Errors

Time of Jacob's Trouble
Book 1: The Four Horsemen   Book 2: Beast
Book 3: Witness   Book 4: The Word
Book 5: Judgment   Book 6: Deceiver
Book 7: False Prophet   Book 8: Satan
Book 9: The Image
Book 10: Jesus the Appearance

Crystal Creek Mysteries
Book 1: Two Dead on Crystal Creek
Book 2: Poison Tea
Book 3: A Latte to Die For
Book 4: Drop Dead Gorgeous

Independent Titles
Adam's Bones
Encounters of the God-Kind
Mercy Reigns: The Millennium
Out of Time: The Vanderbilt Incident
The Forum
The Minister's Haunting
Tomorrow's Promise

1

November, Six Months Earlier

"SECONDS TURN INTO minutes, then hours and days. Weeks pass. Years fly by. Time ticks away our life like rodents devouring cheese." Dorothy Powell tells her therapist, Dr. Archibald.

"Then . . ." her blazing Robin-blue eyes radiate a wildness.

"Then what?" He sits on the edge of his chair, bushy-white eyebrows hiked with interest. "Go on."

"Then," a slice across her throat, "death wins."

"Well, Dorothy, how does that thought make you feel?"

"Feel? Certainly not warm and fuzzy, Dr. Archibald!"

Beady black eyes behind spectacles glare at Dorothy.

"What?"

"Do you need a feel-good pill to help you through the day?"

The laughter escaping her lips is surprising.

"You know, James . . ." The dandruff flies off her Clairol-red hair like snowflakes on blood. "I was truly hoping for more insight than taking a pill. You are, after all, a professional psychic."

"Psychiatrist, Dorothy. There's a huge difference."

"I don't want a double D-D pill!"

"I'm just saying, no need for you to be depressed."

"I'm not!" she snaps at him. "I'm a realist, Dr. Archibald."

"How so?"

"Are you sure you're up for the truth today?"

His lips wiggle. "That's my job, Ms. Powell."

The air between them is crisp with animosity.

"Well, James, truth beknown, this touchy-feeling stuff is pure bullshit. Your probing my mind sets my last nerve on fire!" she exclaims. "In fact, I'm so hot I'm about to go up in flames."

Worry lines crease his forehead, pleasing Dorothy.

"What exactly do you mean?"

"Just this, James. If you don't know me after eight months of therapy, I've paid you far too much." She points a fire-engine manicured nail at him. "So, I really have no other choice."

"We all have choices, Dorothy."

"I'm glad you believe that, Dr. Archibald."

"Why is that?"

"Because, as of this moment, you're fired!"

And just like that Dorothy abandons the couch, walks out of his office and slams the Double D-D door behind her.

This is still America. The land of the free.

Five minutes later, she sits in the back of a Ford sedan. The Uber driver is taking her to the Nashville International Airport.

God willing, when she sees that sneaky CIA Agent Thomas Kessler, she'll squeeze the answers out of him. The last time they'd spoken, over a year ago, he'd asked her to marry him on the banks of Crystal Creek. Then disappeared into the ethers.

Three days ago, Tom had dropped the assassin threat on her by email. "The CIA is going to kill you, Dorothy. You need to get out of the country," he'd warn. "Trust me. I can help you."

Trust you? Only as far as I can throw you, dear.

Glancing at her wristwatch, Dorothy no longer trusts digital time. The phone tucked in her purse is untraceable. A burner. In her time with Tom, she'd learned some tricks of the spy trade.

The internet connects her daughter's cell phone.

"Hi, Mama," Claire says. "Where are you?"

"Driving. I won't be home for a while." It wasn't a lie, although she wasn't driving her car. It was still parked outside the Dr. Archibald's building with a note on the windshield. *Sorry.*

"Did your session with Dr. Archibald go well?" Claire stirs chocolate batter in an aluminum bowl then adds a cup of toasted chopped pecans. Her granddaughter June sits at the bar, salivating over the odor of chocolate mingled with a vanilla flavor.

"Can I speak to GG?" June begs.

"Is that my granddaughter's voice I hear?" Dorothy says.

"Yes, we're making brownies. It's June's time to bring snacks to school for recess." Claire pours the batter in a greased pan.

"Let me talk to GG, please!" June squeals.

"Put June on the phone, Claire."

A moment of shuffling occurs.

"GG, I miss you so much. Come home. We'll half a brownie if Granny will let us." She looks at Claire, anticipating a reaction.

"Maybe another time, June," Dorothy says.

"Oh, shoot. Okay, GG, I'll eat your half of the brownie."

"Listen to your grandmother, June. Claire will teach you how to cook. You'll grow up to be a fine lady with culinary skills."

"GG, that's adult talk I don't understand. Goodbye."

Plunk.

"Sorry, Mama." Claire picks up the cell phone.

"No problem." Dorothy chuckles. June is razor smart with a no-nonsense tongue as sharp as her great-grandmother's.

Claire says. "So . . . the therapy session?"

"I've had all the advice I can stomach in a lifetime."

"Are you certain?" Claire places the brownies in the oven to bake. "I thought Dr. Archibald was helping you deal with your difficult past." The CIA had made her mother appear insane.

"He didn't, but I'm okay with that."

"Which makes me wonder why, Mama."

"God works in mysterious ways, dear. American citizens have rights. We are His eyes, hands, and feet. It's our duty to see that justice wins over evil and corruption. I'm His soldier."

"Mama, you're scaring me," Claire utters. "You're starting to sound like Thomas Kessler. Have you heard from him?"

"He's always a ghost in the wind!" Dorothy blows a red curl off her forehead. "I know, I've been such a fool for love."

"Come on home, Mama. We'll talk about what's bothering you." Claire dries her wet hands with a tea towel.

"Talk won't help. I know you're glad I didn't marry Tom. You think he's too young for me. And far too dangerous."

"No, I think you are too wise for him—with a few years to boot," Claire exclaims. "I hope you never see the cad again."

Dorothy chuckles. "That was tactful, daughter."

"I just want what's best for you, Mama. You've had enough stress for one lifetime." Claire leans elbows on the bar.

"I really appreciate all you've done for me, dear."

"Tom is dangerous, Mama. He kidnapped you and dragged you across the continent to recapture millions of dollars?"

"U. S. dollars the Russian Mafia stole from America."

"It wasn't your responsibility to collect the funds."

"I know, Claire. But I had fun, so I'm not sorry about my adventure. Tom saved me from grief. I'd walk through fire for him." *If I don't kill him first.* "I was desperate to reinvent my life."

"Desperate measures for desperate people." Claire groans.

"Exactly! Which sounds like a line in a novel."

"I read the book notes you left locked in the bedside stand. Forget about publishing, Mama, you're stirring the flames."

"Goodness, Claire! Locks mean Don't Touch.'"

"The CIA is a disturbing force in the world," Claire points out. "They have power behind their punch. What do you have?"

"The truth, Claire. It's important I tell my story. People need know they can't trust spooks. If not to inform others about the nature of spying, I need to write the book to please myself."

"Too dangerous, Mama. The feds cherish their secrets."

"So do I, Claire. We have a plan."

"*We?* You and Tom? That's even scarier, Mama."

"Don't you worry your pretty head; I have skills now."

"We'll talk more about this when you get home."

"I don't think so, Claire."

2

April, the Following Year

"LORENE, THIS IS Claire Burkes."

"Oh, hi, Claire. Have you heard from our girl?"

"Not exactly." Claire knew that's how Lorene Perkins referred to her mother. They were Canasta partners every Friday at the Columbia Senior Citizen Center. The card game that had been going on for decades starts at 2 p.m. Lorene Perkins is always her mother's partner opposing Lizzy Hinson and Jane Murphy. Nobody stops the game. *Ever.* Under any circumstances.

"Either you have heard from Dorothy or you haven't."

Claire blinks back tears. There's no good way to say it.

"Mama's gone." She chokes out her words over the phone.

"I know—wait! Dorothy came home without telling me?"

"No, she didn't. Something bad has happened."

"Don't tell me she wrecked her practically new Cadillac!" Lorene rocks the swing on the back porch of her Maury County two-story country home. Sipping on a glass of cold sweet tea to keep cool, May weather has taken root heading toward summer.

"What?" Claire's conversation with her mother's best friend always feels like wading through glue. There truly is a social gap between generations no sane human can leap over.

"If Dorothy had a wreck, her insurance will go sky-high."

"Lorene . . ." might as well say it, "Mama died."

"She *cried?* Lordy, did Thomas Kessler break her heart again?" Lorene's response catches Claire off guard.

"Uh, I don't know the details." Sadness feels like a cloak over Claire's face, choking the life out of her. She can barely breathe.

"You should take her car keys away. Dorothy drives like a maniac. And those drugs the therapist gave her?"

"Shut up, Lorene, and listen to me!" Claire is done with foolish banter. "I received an email from Tom a little while ago."

"I hope you hung up on him, he's big trouble."

"It was email, Lorene. He's sending Mama's ashes."

"He's a lying piece of trash, Claire. Dorothy doesn't smoke."

"Lorene!" No way, but to say it! "Mama was cremated."

"I don't believe it, Claire. Dorothy would not die without telling me first." Lorene mulls over Claire's statement.

"Actually, I don't know what to believe," Claire admits.

"Well, I do. Tom is lying. He's probably on the other side of the world with Dorothy on some clandestine mission."

"You really believe Mama's alive?"

"No way to know for sure unless we investigate."

"You sound just like my mother!" Claire's hope rises for the first time since the email came an hour ago.

"Darn toot'in! You ought' a talk to my daughter-in-law about testing those ashes for Dorothy's DNA. Nothing sneaky gets past Cyn." Dr. Cynthia Perkins is the Maury County coroner.

"That's a good idea, Lorene. Mama's ossuary with the ashes is due to arrive at the Johnson's Funeral Home next Friday," Claire reports. "Maybe Graham can ask Cyn to test the ashes for me."

"I'll do better 'n that, I'll call Cyn and ask her myself."

Claire chuckles. *Cyn* makes her think of sin.

"Thanks, Lorene, you're a good friend to Mama."

"I'll let you know what she says," Lorene utters. "Meanwhile, I've got to find a substitute for our Canasta game on Friday."

"When did you last hear from Mama?" Claire asks.

"Not since early February. She wrote."

"What did she say?" Claire inquires.

"That she was busy, and she'd let me know when she's coming home," Lorene replies. "Is that important?"

"How did she sound in the letter?"

"Like she was having fun," Lorene replies. "Busy joyful people don't have time to die, Claire."

"Okay, I guess you're right. Thanks for encouraging me."

"Our job as the older generation, girl. You make your mother proud!" Lorene spouts. "Just keep your chin up, okay?"

"I will," Claire says and ends the call.

* * *

Claire's news is troubling. Lorene is not sad, she's mad!

I refuse to accept Dorothy is dead.

If Dorothy believed she was in danger, wouldn't she have written or phoned? The Canasta Club girls always had each other's backs. Lorene opens the screen door to her house and enters.

A few minutes later, she's in her bedroom dressing to leave the house. "No way my friend is dead!" she voices.

Dorothy Powell's tragic life can't possibly end before she tells her side of the story to the public. The CIA had used her, abused her, then locked her up in a mental hospital. If she is dead by the hands of a hired assassin, there will be no victory to celebrate at her memorial service. Only profound sadness.

Lorene grabs her purse and jaunts through the den, thinking of how the melodrama had begun six years ago, before both their husbands were murdered on the banks of Crystal Creek. Dorothy had become bent on finding their killer. Then Thomas Kessler showed up at the Senior Citizen Center as the acting director.

He cooed and wooed the sad widow.

What Dorothy didn't know was Tom moved to Columbia to spy on her for the CIA. He captured Dorothy's affections to accomplish his own damn agenda. She was a fool for love.

"Oh well . . ." Lorene sighs and gets in her pea-green Tesla. She's on a mission this morning. The other girls in the club need to know what Claire said. Lizzy Hinson will be her first stop.

On her way over, she phones Jane Murphy.

3

AFTER PARKING IN Lizzy' Hinson's driveway, Lorene mounts the covered porch and bangs on the door. Three times to gain Lizzy's attention. Then tests the doorknob.

Unlocked.

She trots over to the nearest window.

No view there.

The curtains are drawn in the living room to keep out the rising heat. But there's a light on beyond the door leading to the den. No choice but to open the door and step inside.

Lorene enters, pauses and listens.

No sounds other than the limpid AC air blowing through the floor vents. The atmosphere is stuffy with kitchen odors. Lizzy had a hamburger for last night's supper. A recently baked cake.

For a moment, Lorene feels like an intruder.

Perspiration breaks out under her arms. It's far too warm inside the house. Although Lizzy can well afford it, she's too cheap, or maybe energy-conscientious, to put her AC on 74.

The wood floors creak as Lorene walks down a short hallway separating the living area from a formal dining room.

She stops at the doorway, peeking into the den.

"Lizzy?"

Nothing.

Lizzy has to be in the house. She left the front door open.

Lorene calls out louder to her friend.

No response.

Then takes three steps forward and listens.

"Lizzy?"

"Is that a real person or my TV?"

Aw, success!

"It's me, Lizzy." Lorene follows the voice through the kitchen and down a short hallway toward the master bedroom wing added on two years ago when Graham built his house.

She stops short of the guest half-bath next to the laundry room, also enlarged when the bedroom wing was built.

"It's me, Lizzy," Lorene calls out.

"Okay, Me, I'm in here on the potty."

Lorene pushes open the bathroom door and stares down.

"Goodness, girl, you stink?" She flips on the overhead fan. "Did you have to take Milk of Magnesia?"

The younger senior by three years is hunched over, seated on the commode holding her stomach tightly as if straining.

"Are you in pain?" Lorene asks, holding her nose.

Lizzy glances up. "You might've knocked before barging in."

"I did knock, and I did call out to you. Is your AC broken?"

"No." Lizzy wipes, stands, and pulls up her pants.

"Are those Depends?" Lorene giggles.

Lizzy bends over and flushes the commode.

"A semi version. Please don't tell the other girls."

Lorene knows she's referring to Dorothy and Jane.

"Did I invite you over?" Lizzy tries to recall, leading the way back down the hall and into the kitchen.

"No, I invited myself over," Lorene answers.

"I didn't hear you knock."

"Well, I did. Umpteen times. Your front door was unlocked. Why put in a security system if you don't lock your doors, Lizzy?"

"Don't lecture me, friend. I opened the front door to get my package from the Fed-Ex guy. Laxative was calling and I didn't have time to lock the door back or set the alarm again."

"Goodness, girl! If I'd been a burglar—or God forbid, a serial killer—who knows what might have happened if I hadn't shown up?" Lorene wags her head. "You have to be more careful."

"Girls! Where are you?" a lyrical voice drifts from the ethers.

Lizzy frowns and glares at Lorene. "You invited Jane over without telling me? Is this your birthday and I forgot it?"

"No, and stop asking so many questions, Lizzy."

A gaunt elongated face with the appearance of white crinkled tissue paper peeks around the doorjamb to the den, leaving the rest of her body to wonder about. Faded blue eyes magnified by a pair of pink-rimmed glasses find what they seek.

"Oh, there you two are!" Jane steps into full view.

"What are you doing here, Jane?" Lizzy queries.

"I dropped everything to rush over here when Lorene called. Did I miss somebody's birthday?" She inhales cake odors. "What's going on, girls? Another mystery we need to solve?"

"Ask Lorene. She showed up ten minutes ago."

Lorene groans. She's about to burst Jane's happy bubble with her news. "I always have a reason for breaking into a house."

"Okay, spit it out!" Lizzy pipes. "This is ridiculous!"

Lorene jerks a breath and looks at her friends. She needs to somehow soften the blow before telling the girls about Dorothy's ashes due to arrive at the funeral home on Friday.

"I'm actually thirsty, Lizzy. May I have a glass of water?"

"Sure. I also have tea and sodas. Have a seat at the bar, girls." Lizzy says as she looks at Jane. "What about you?"

"I'll have a diet soda if it's no trouble."

"No trouble at all for friends." Lizzy fills three plastic tumblers with ice cubes in preparation to add their drinks. She feels much better now that the laxative has cleaned out her gut, but it's left her as dehydrated as a camel crossing a desert.

"Water, Lorene?" She uncaps a bottle of purified water.

"You don't trust Columbia's water source?" Jane alerts to a problem. "What's wrong with your tap water? Is it contaminated by that new car factory that just went in east of Columbia?"

"Nothing is wrong with anything, Jane," Lizzy says.

"Do you have dessert?" Lorene inquires. "I had a late breakfast and no lunch." Delay, delay, delay the news.

Jane looks at her Mickey Mouse wristwatch on her right arm. It was a Christmas gift from her granddaughter Susie.

"Are you in a hurry, Jane?" Lorene inquires.

"I can't stay long, I'm due for a stomach pill at three."

Always meds for the elderly, Lorene inwardly groans.

"Forget about those blame pills, Jane," Lizzy pipes. "I baked Granny's chocolate cake recipe this morning. Took me over two hours of prep." She beams. "Too much to eat by myself."

"That sounds lovely, Lizzy," Lorene says.

"Well, I will stay long enough to enjoy a slice of your grandmother's chocolate cake recipe with a scoop of vanilla ice cream." Jane deposits her purse on the floor as she perches on a barstool. "I'll have a cup of coffee instead of a soda."

"Wonderful, ladies!" Lizzy dumps out the glass of diet Pepsi and removes the Maxwell House coffee from the cabinet.

Lorene decides on coffee, too, with a glass of water, grateful for the opportunity to delay the awful news Claire dumped on her earlier that day. The four of them are soul sisters.

"I admire you, Lizzy. You've always been the hostess with the mostess! I didn't inherit the cooking gene," Jane says. "Kroger pastries are the best I can do for my guests. But my daughter caught the gene from my grandmother on my daddy's side."

Bravo Jane, let's talk about your side of the family.

"That's sweet, Jane." The odor of perking coffee permeates the kitchen as Lizzy starts slicing the cake. Then pauses.

"Lorene? Why this sudden get-to-gather?" Jane looks at Lizzy, who only shrugs. She doesn't know, either.

The lump in Lorene's dry throat garbles her words.

Huh? "What did you say?" Lizzy asks.

"I—uh." Lorene dreads sharing her bad news. Maybe it was a mistake coming here. She should've just called and dropped the Dorothy bomb. They are going to be so upset . . .

I can't do this. Lorene picks up her purse to leave.

"Wait! Is this about Dorothy? Will she be home by Friday?" Jane inquires, glaring at Lizzy. "Is there something wrong"

"We need a replacement for our Canasta game on Friday," Lorene replies. "Dorothy might never be coming home."

4

CLAIRE TALKED TO Lorene Perkins an hour ago and told her what Thomas Kessler wrote in his email. Somehow, dingy Lorene had encouraged her not to accept the terrible news without first verifying the facts. When the back door suddenly opens, she alerts to danger. There have been recent break-ins in the neighborhood.

"What are you doing here, Theodore?"

He closes the door and takes a few steps toward Claire.

"So, now you're calling me Theodore and not Ted?"

"Let's not pretend we are on friendly terms." Ted slumps over to the bar as Claire places a dirty glass in the dishwasher.

"Was I expecting you this afternoon?"

"Nope. Dropped by to pick up a summer suit I forgot to pack," he answers. "You should keep your doors locked."

"I should do a lot of things, Theodore, but you don't live here anymore, so you have no right to give me advice."

"I see . . . you just can't be nice."

"Nope. You should've called first. I might've been busy."

They had been separated for three months. Ted was spending more time with Darlene than at home. If he wanted to shack up with his beautiful young assistant attorney, let him. Marriage isn't working for us. After his bastard son was born, Ted started paying for her apartment, claiming she needed financial help. Diapers and baby food and formula costs through the roof.

Why pay for Theodore's mistakes?

"As if you work a job, Claire." Ted loosens his tight necktie.

His crinkled spring suit fits too snuggly and his brown loafers are scuffed. Darlene doesn't shine them like she had. Ted always had trouble pushing away from the table. He's a walking recipe for an early heart attack. Not that she cares a whit anymore.

Ted grits his teeth. "I should get my suit and go."

"You do that, Theodore. And put that witch on birth control, for God's sake. She won't get another dime, if I have my way."

Marriage counseling had miserably failed.

"I forgot how truly vindictive you can be, Claire."

"And I forgot you were a cheating liar, so we're even."

They both tired of the banter and didn't want to fight. Ted had hired a lawyer outside his firm to negotiate a settlement with Claire in lieu of a pending divorce. He didn't want it, but she was unforgiving, unrelenting, and bent on taking him to the cleaners.

Claire notes the fatigue in Ted's sagging face mixed with something like defeat, or maybe depression. He looks old.

"You look tired, Ted. Does Darlene make you get up to feed Jamie?" The words were out of her mouth before she knew it.

"You don't look so good, either, Claire. Are you sick?"

"I wish. You can take a pill for that." She drops her butt on the sofa, leans over and places her head in a pair of shaky hands.

"What's wrong?"

"I've had a terrible day."

He limps over and sits down by Claire, fondly pushing her short blond curls out of the path of her sight.

"Is June or Billy sick? Did he have a football accident?"

She glances up, stunned by his empathy.

Don't touch, or I might just give you a hug.

"Why have you been crying?"

Claire sits up straight and looks at him.

"I'm sad, Ted. About what's happened to us and other things." Is she ready to tell him his favorite mother-in-law died? "Mama warned me not to marry you and I just did not listen."

"Well, that's a one-eighty." He chuckles.

"Nothing is funny today, Ted."

"Good thing you didn't listen to Dorothy or Ben and Helen would not be breathing. Plus, you love our grandkids. June and Billy are shining stars in our lives. Are they mistakes, too?"

At hearing his words, Claire's blue eyes blaze with tears. How can she win an argument against an experienced defense attorney?

If he cheats on her, is he conning the IRS, too? Maybe he launders the money for the rich-and-famous Nashville country stars.

Ted knows exactly what to say to get to me.

If she forgives him, he'll just waltz right back into her life and take up residency. She can't let him have his cake and eat it, too.

"Just saying, sweetheart." Ted fondly touches Claire's hand.

"Don't you dare call me that!" Claire jerks away.

"Our marriage does not have to end like this, Claire. You know I still love you. I'm just trying to do the right thing."

"Something you should have thought about before you got Darlene pregnant," Claire coldly states the fact.

"I confessed and said I was sorry," he defends himself.

"A thousand apologies wouldn't matter. I'm just not in a place to forgive." She glances away to hide her pain.

"I wouldn't have moved out if you hadn't been so dadgum difficult about my supporting Darlene financially after Jamie was born." If looks could kill him, he was already dead.

"Well, thank God I grew some balls and put my foot down."

"Claire, I'm tired. I'll get my stuff and go."

As he got up from the sofa, she peeps, "Mama died."

Slowly, Ted turns around and glares down.

"Dorothy's too mean to die."

"You always disliked her," Claire says.

"Dorothy never made it easy for me."

"That doesn't matter now."

"Why not?"

"I received an email from Thomas Kessler this morning. He's sending Mama's ashes to Johnson's Funeral Home. They are due to arrive this Friday. I have to plan her—" she chokes.

"He had her body cremated without asking you!" Ted thinks about it. "You're sure someone didn't hack your email?"

"I hadn't thought of that, Ted. Lorene wants me to have the ashes tested for DNA. Dr. Cynthia Perkins is the coroner for Maury County. Cyn's married to Lorene's son, Graham."

"Cremation destroys human tissue, Claire."

"Lorene says her daughter-in-law is really smart. If anything isn't up to snuff with the ashes, she can find it."

"And you trust Lorene's judgment?"

"I have to know if the ashes belong to my mother."

"Maybe you should just plan a memorial service."

"Lorene knows Mama better than anyone else. If she thinks my mother is still alive, then maybe I should, too."

"I'm sorry, Claire. I don't know how I can help."

"What?"

"I take that back." He stares. "If you need an attorney to sort out Dorothy's will-and-testament, you know how to reach me."

"How very kind of you," Claire sarcastically remarks.

"I'm going now." He starts for the door.

Don't bother coming back, Claire mouths.

After Ted had gone, she folds the dry clothes in the laundry room. If only she could turn time back and do things differently. She would be more loving to Ted. More understanding of his passion for the law. Perhaps, even more forgiving.

But, it's too late now.

As Shakespeare had said: *The dye is cast.*

5

"I SUGGEST WE invite Jessica Bailey to replace Dorothy at our Canasta game on Friday," Jane says. "She's new in town."

"Is she a widow like us?" Lizzy asks, removing their dirty dishes from the bar and placing them in the kitchen sink.

"Jess's husband is a retired doctor from Knoxville."

"I know a lot of people who would be glad to fill in for Dorothy, now that Loretta quit and moved to Nashville."

Lorene tells Lizzy, "Better to ask a stranger to play with us than a good friend. We don't won't to hurt anyone's feelings."

Jane adds, "I had a long conversation with Jess and she's lonely. She's been dealing with losing her daughter from cancer recently. It would be the kind neighborly thing to include her."

Lorene could readily identify with that stress since her daughter Jenny had fought off breast cancer a few years back.

"I suppose it will be the Christian thing to do, to befriend Jess," Lizzy agrees. "But we should let her know it's only temporary—till Dorothy gets home." Her gaze wanders.

"Agreed, girls?" Jane smiles.

"Agreed," Lorene concurs.

"Well, the chocolate cake was delicious, Lizzy." Jane had wanted to lick her plate clean. "But I have to go home now."

"Your pills call," Lizzy teases.

"Wait, Jane. Before you leave, I have to tell you something," Lorene can no longer delay her awful news about Dorothy.

"You sound serious, girl," Lizzy utters.

"Claire Burkes called me a little while ago with some news."

"Good or bad news?"

"Depends on how you view it," Lorene says.

"I don't understand," Jane states.

"Me, either," Lizzy chimes in. "Don't leave us hanging."

"What did Claire say?" Jane asks, looking at her watch.

"That she received an email from Thomas Kessler."

"Did that cad kidnap our girl again?" Lizzy fusses.

"I swear I could squeeze that weasel's neck for the way he's treated Dorothy!" Jane exclaims. "Tom's nothing but trouble!"

Lorene looks at Lizzy. "Not this time, girls."

"Spill it, Lorene!" Jane demands. "I'm on a timetable."

"Dorothy's ashes are arriving at Johnson Funeral Home this Friday," Lorene reveals. "I thought you should know."

"That's silly, she never smoked!" Lizzy rolls her eyes.

Lorene grins. "Exactly my response when Claire called."

"Why can't you tell us what is both good and bad?"

"Okay, Lizzy, I give in. Tom emailed that he was shipping an ossuary with Dorothy's ashes to the funeral home for burial. Our girl has died—or so he claims. That's the bad news."

"So, what's the good?" Jane wonders.

"I don't believe a word he wrote to Claire."

"So, Dorothy isn't dead?" Lizzy pokes a finger in one ear.

"That's our job to find out," Lorene concludes.

They talk another few minutes then part ways.

Lorene is home by 4:30 p.m. She watches Graham's house from her back porch in anticipation of Cyn's car pulling into their garage at five. She'd decided it was best to go over and talk to her, rather than phone in her news about Dorothy's ashes. When her daughter-in-law pulls into the garage, she walks over.

She knocks on the front door and waits. Soon, Lorene hears footfalls on the wood floors before the door opens.

"Mama? What are you doing here?"

"Do you have a moment, Cyn?"

"Sure. Come in, you look flustered."

"I am flustered, dear. I received some really bad news earlier today." She limps over to the sofa and plops down.

"I'm so sorry, can I get you something to drink?"

"Yes, water, please."

"Graham is working late tonight at the pharmacy," Cyn reveals. "Would you like to have supper with me?"

"Sure." Lorene had not thought about eating since she'd talked to the other girls. "Where is my granddaughter?"

"Alicia is staying with my mother for a few days." Cyn walks into the kitchen and removes a pan from the fridge freezer. "I just need to thaw out the zucchini with chicken and pasta."

"Fine, I'm in no hurry. I have no plans for tonight."

Lorene delays making her request until she's so sleepy she has to go home and go to bed. "Cyn, I need a favor from you."

"Sure. What kind of favor, Mama?"

"It's rumored a close friend has died. Her ashes are due to arrive at Johnson Funeral Home on Friday."

"What do you want me to do about that, Mama?"

"Can you perform a DNA test on the ashes?"

"Why?"

"What if the remains aren't my friend's?"

"Who are you talking about, Mama?"

"Dorothy Powell. I don't trust the source of the rumor."

Cyn's dark eyelashes flutter. "Has an order been placed?"

Lorene frowns. "What kind of order?"

"I can't perform any kind of test without a court order signed by a local judge," Cyn says. "There are rules for human remains."

"Oh, I didn't know that. Well, can't you just do it as a favor to me without telling anyone?" Lorene cares nothing for protocol.

"No, Mama. Not without risking my job."

"We all take risks every day, Cynthia."

"I won't do it without legal authorization."

"Will you ask somebody else to do it for me, Cyn?"

"No, Mama."

"It will be our secret."

The back door opens and steps inside. "Hi, Mama."

"Hi, son."

"What are you doing here at this late hour? Are you sick?"

"No, son. I'm solving a huge problem."

He laughs. "Far from me to interfere."

6

Six Months Ago

TWO DAYS AFTER Dorothy flew to Dallas, Texas, she anxiously sits at a wrought-iron table outside a popular downtown bistro. It's crazy to trust anyone associated with the CIA.

But she waits anyhow. Who else has her back? She hones in on a handsome man nearly two decades her junior. The cad who proposed marriage to her a year ago, then fell off her radar.

Until he contacted her with a cryptic warning.

"Hi, honey. I'm late. Please don't be mad."

Dorothy's date pulls out a chair and sits across from her.

Huge puppy-brown eyes fondly sweep over her. They possess a glitter reflecting high intelligence. His thick gray hair is coiffured, making her feel like a lost Cinderella before she is presented with a pair of glittering shoes. Going limp, every fiber in her body fights to resist Thomas Kessler's charming smile and personality.

Double D-D! She'd rather give him a year's worth of her opinion that he's a piece of you-know-what! But she's bent on keeping this conversation civil. Calmly, she peers at him.

"I'm not mad, Tom, just disappointed."

His grin is disarming.

"Good. Where's the engagement ring I gave you?"

"That thing—I threw it away." She rolls her blue eyes.

"Don't do that, honey."

"What? The sensible thing any sane person would do?"

"When were you ever a sensible person?"

To that, Dorothy has no argument.

"You know that I love you, honey."

"Quit calling me honey!" Angst rises in Dorothy like an angry riptide. "What I do know is that you're a liar!" she hisses.

Forget civility! We're already past that.

Tom rears back in his chair, studies her like a creepy spider that reflects his true spy nature. Then shakes his head.

"I'm sorry I left the states without telling you."

"Choices have consequences, Tom."

"My life went off the rails after we last spoke."

Dorothy glances away to hide her tears.

"So . . . you just abandoned me?" She's still in love with him, regardless of the fact he'd proposed marriage on the banks of Crystal Creek then not one word or call. Until recently.

"Please let me explain, honey."

Inhaling deeply, she makes firm eye contact.

"Okay, I'm listening, where were you?"

"Locked up in a damn Russian prison."

"No profanity, please. God doesn't like that."

He laughs again. "I expect I'm not His favorite, either."

She haughtily laughs. "A statement of truth, I'm surprised."

He leans firm muscular arms on the table. "Honey—"

"Don't call me that, Tom, I'm not your honey! We're not engaged anymore. And the only reason I'm here is to say goodbye. Permanently." She slams a fist on the table, jarring the cup of coffee between them until it leaps and splatters over his shirt.

She actually laughs, feeling some vindication.

Shocked, Tom grabs a wad of napkins to wipe the foam from his sea-green shirt that probably costs more than Dorothy's whole outfit—which consists of a pair of casual slacks and light sweater.

"Now, look what you've gone and done."

Satisfaction comes in many packages. The look on Tom's face is rewarding. For a nanosecond, she feels sorry for him, but that doesn't last. Dorothy is purpose-driven, and here only to find out why her former fiancé believes she is in immediate danger.

"Why were you incarcerated in Moscow?"

"Yeah, CIA switched me out for another agent they felt was more worthy," he explains. "When I gave nothing up, some

Russian thugs unlocked my bars late one night and took me out to a deserted location to—" he mimicked a slash across his neck.

"You're too mean to die," Dorothy says.

"Actually, I got shot and almost did." He unbuttons his shirt. There's a scar on his chest where a bullet wound had healed.

"A farmer found me and took care of me. I was out of it for three days before I woke up. The bullet just missed my heart."

"Lucky miss for you." She's intrigued by his elaborate tale. Actually, if she recalls, that scar was already there three years ago when they first took off to Europe to rob international banks.

Tom grins. "You don't believe me."

"Not one iota, but I've been in prison, too."

"I heard . . . a mental institution."

"You heard? Why didn't you send someone to help me?" Another burst of unrestrained anger beyond her control.

"I couldn't, Dorothy. Prisons have locked doors."

"I hate you, Thomas Kessler!"

Calmly, he grins. "Love does funny things to people."

"I don't suppose you knew the CIA was going to give me drugs, then declare me insane. It must have been LSD because I had so many visions that weren't true. It was hell, Tom."

"For that, I'm truly sorry, but I've been busy."

"Okay, doing what?"

"After leaving Russia, I went to Afghanistan."

"Doing what?"

"I posed as a Muslim so I could spy on America's enemy, hoping to regain the CIA's graces," Tom explains.

"You're too white to fool the Arabs."

"Trust me, I was armed with information they wanted."

"You fed them false information so that the CIA gained an advantage in catching some of their key Muslim leaders."

"You're too smart for your britches, woman. Why don't we get married and I'll take them off? After a good spanking, we'll see where that leads." His quick witty tongue shocks Dorothy.

But to her chagrin, it sounds pretty enticing.

Be sensible, you naughty girl.

"This conversation is over, Tom. Goodbye."

Dorothy stands to leave when Tom grabs her arm and pulls her into an embrace. "Not yet, Nancy Drew, you have a problem." The next instant they are madly kissing in public.

"What was that for?" she asks.

"To remind you of what you will be leaving behind."

She rubs her lips, feeling a bit tipsy.

"What's wrong, Dorothy?"

"I, uh—wasn't totally convinced."

"Okay, happy to try that again."

This kiss is all that he'd promised. Finally, Dorothy comes up for air, sighing and wondering what had possessed her to leave.

Tom grins. "Was that better, darling?"

"I'm getting there, you bad boy!"

7

The Present

IT'S FRIDAY, 2 P.M. The square table on the back patio of the Columbia Senior Citizen seats four Canasta players. Jane Murphy, a retired librarian, is Jessica Bailey's partner, the newcomer to town. Lorene Perkins, a graduate of Vanderbilt, will parlay with Elizabeth Hinson, a retired elementary school teacher.

As rapid conversations ensue, Lorene deals the first round of cards in their game. Jane, seated to Lorene's left, will play first. After organizing her thirteen cards, she turns up three red threes before drawing four more cards. If her team gets one more red three, they will earn 100 bonus points. Jane discards a card.

It's Lizzy's turn to draw. She turns up the fourth red three.

Jane frowns at Jessica, her partner. "I tried," she mouths. No one will earn 800 points this round for getting all four red threes.

Grinning, Lizzy draws two cards and discards one.

Jess takes her turn then it's Lorene's time to play.

"Well, Jess, what brought you to Columbia?" Lorene asks as she draws her two cards and studies her hand before discarding.

"John retired from a clinic in Atlanta—he was a pediatrician." Jess's eyes skitter to the other girls at the table. "Our daughter was sick—cancer." She paused to collect her emotions.

"Well..." Lizzy pats Jess's hand, "we're so sorry about your daughter's, uh—" she couldn't bring herself to say the word death.

Tears gather in Jess's gaze. "Death is really hard."

"Yes, it is," Jane adds. "We recently lost a good friend."

"Dorothy Powell," Lorene says. "Her ashes are due at the funeral home sometime today. I need to call her daughter Claire after our game is over and see where we are with—" she stops.

"With what?" Jess asks, drying her wet cheeks.

"Well, when Claire and I last spoke, I suggested my daughter-in-law perform a DNA test on Dorothy's ashes," Lorene reveals.

"You question if Dorothy is dead?" Jess employs wild cards to close two seven-card suits. "Is there a reason you think that?"

"More hanky-panky goes on in Columbia than you ever want to know," Lizzy quips. "News of her death was awful sudden."

"Let's talk about something else," Lorene suggests. They don't know Jess all that well to include her in their investigation.

Jane can't help herself as she utters, "We can't actually trust the person who reported Dorothy's death to her daughter."

"If the ashes don't belong to Dorothy, we'll find out."

Jess looks at Jane. "How old is Dorothy?"

"Eighty-six, but she had a face-lift," Lizzy reveals.

"She looks twenty years younger—beautiful. We should all have some of our wrinkles cut away," Jane says, longingly.

"A face lift is expensive," Lizzy points out. "But Dorothy didn't have to worry about money after she collected that huge insurance policy after Arthur died." She plays her card hand.

"Girls!" Lorene hails. "We're confusing our new friend. Let's finish our Canasta game and I'll fill her in on the details later."

"Agreed," Jane and Lizzy say.

So, the game goes on, as ever . . .

They finish up at 4:20 p.m. and stow the cards in the cabinet for another day. Goodbyes are short because everyone is tired.

Lorene is on her way out the front door when Jess catches up with her. "Do you have supper plans for tonight?"

"On a Friday?" Lorene stops walking and faces Jess. "Like, I have a hot date tonight?" She chuckles. "I wish . . ."

"Well, I won't go as far as that . . ." Jess teases.

"No plans. What do you have in mind?"

"Let me buy you supper?"

"Sure." Lorene opens the front door for Jess. "What about John? Will he join us?" The sweltering day's heat hits them.

"Leave your car here." Jess pops the locks to her dark blue Mercedes. "John's playing cards tonight with some new friends."

Lorene fills the passenger side of the Mercedes and Jess takes the driver's seat and turns on the AC. She is suspicious of Jess's spontaneous invitation to supper. Perhaps Jane and Lizzy's comments regarding Dorothy's ashes spurred the invitation.

Regardless, it's nice not to go home to an empty house and eat alone. "Where do you suggest we dine?" Lorene asks.

"You choose." Jess drives the sedan down the street. "John and I have been too busy unpacking our stuff in our new home to check out the local restaurants. You must have a preference."

"Do you like barbeque?"

"Love it. Tell me how to get there?"

Bark's Seared Pork is located a few blocks from downtown Columbia. Jess handily follows Lorene's directions. It's still early, so they find a parking place near the entrance. They get out.

Jess locks the car and they enter the front door. Charlie Bark, the owner, greets them. He flirts a few minutes with Jess, like he always did with Dorothy. Charlie has a flair with the women that makes them smile and keeps them dining at his establishment.

Judy, the new waitress, shows them to a table by a window.

"Dorothy and I used to come here often." Lorene snags a laminated menu and nervously fiddles with it. She doesn't trust newcomers, so she must be careful sharing information about Dorothy's life. Jane likes her, so maybe Jess is an okay person.

"Dorothy was your best friend." Jess snaps a thick paper napkin across her lap. Charlie has the large kind to catch spills.

"I love Jane and Lizzy, but yes, Dorothy and I were especially close. Our husbands were both murdered by the same assassin."

"That's awful!" Jess says as she studies her menu choices. "What do you usually order?" She looks to Lorene for a decision.

"The barbeque platter is to die for." Lorene's face reddens, feeling like egg is on her face. "Sorry, wrong analogy."

Jess sets the menu aside. "Should I be afraid?"

The question stuns Lorene. "For living here?"

"I've read some of the old news articles at the public library about the murders. Seems to me for a small town like Columbia, the community has had its unfair share of crimes." Jess smacks her lips. "Why was your husband targeted by an assassin?"

"Crawford and Arthur Powell were good friends and played Poker together with several locals every Friday night. A man that played with them told them a secret that made them a target."

"I'm sorry, Lorene." Jess could identify with the idea of getting caught up in a scenario that was less than desirable.

"Me, too. After that, there were other murders."

"Did your husband play poker with the mayor?"

"Yes," Lorene replies. "Why do you ask?"

"John is probably playing with the same group of men tonight." She smiles. "Does that include Bubba the barber?"

"Yes, and other important politicians," Lorene states.

They take a moment to study their menus.

"How did Dorothy become involved with danger?"

"Her trouble came later when Clint Howard moved to Columbia to manage the Senior Citizen Center," Lorene explains. "By then, both our husbands were in the ground. Clint hit on her." Lorene shakes her head. "Dorothy fell hard for him."

"Really? How old was Dorothy at the time?"

"Approaching eighty-two. She was lonely. And didn't have a chance with Clint. Which I might add wasn't his real name."

"Oh, my, this sounds like a soap opera."

"More like a book." Which Dorothy is writing, but Lorene won't tell Jess. "Clint involved Dorothy in some nasty stuff that almost got her killed." And that was all Lorene would say.

Jess paused, looking hard at Lorene.

"Do you believe Dorothy was murdered?"

"I don't even want to believe she is dead," Lorene says.

"So . . . you are out to prove she is alive?"

"If you knew the whole story, you'd wonder, too."

8

CLAIRE HAD SPENT the Friday afternoon seated in Judge James Sewell's office waiting for him to get out of court. He knew her mother well, had even once sentenced her to a night in jail until she'd bailed her out. Detective Lloyd Peters, Butch to her, had arrested her mother for murdering her daddy. None of that was true, but it took time to prove Arthur's widow was innocent.

"Is he actually coming back to the office?" Claire signs.

"Said he was." Secretary Sue Ann pops her bubble gum.

Claire looks at the wall clock. "It's after 4:30 p.m."

"Takes time to shed his cloak. He sometimes showers before coming back," Sue Ann adds. "You can leave him a message."

"No, I need to speak to him directly," Claire insists.

"Speak to me about what?" Judge Sewell appears in the open doorway, one foot still in the hall. "Can this wait till Monday?"

"No, Judge, it's about my mother."

"What did Dorothy do now?"

"Can we discuss this privately in your office?" Sue Ann has a habit of letting the cat out of the bag on FACEBOOK. Claire prefers to keep her mother's death from becoming public.

"You can go now, Sue Ann. I'll lock up."

"Thank you, Judge." She tosses Claire a stare.

When the office door is shut, Claire says, "I need a court order for Dr. Cynthia Preston to examine my mother's ashes."

The judge drops in a chair. "Dorothy's dead."

"Yes. Maybe. I don't know."

He grins. "That's three answers in short form."

"I know . . ." Claire sits across from James' desk.

"How did Dorothy die?"

"I don't know. I was notified by email on Wednesday her cremated ashes would arrive today at Johnson Funeral Home."

"Have you received notification?" James inquires.

"No," Claire replies. "Lorene Perkins questions if the ashes are really my mother's." She stares at the attorney.

"So, that's why you're requesting a DNA test." He nods. "Cremation destroys any signs of human remains, Claire."

"So, I've been told, but I have to try."

"What makes you suspicious the ashes aren't Dorothy's?"

"Since my daddy was murdered, Mama has been targeted and manipulated by a CIA agent—I can't go into details, sorry."

"I see . . ." Judge Sewell taps a pen on his desk, scratches the stubbles on his chin, and rears back, mulling over the request.

Claire becomes hopeful James will agree.

James' best feature is his beady-black eyes that strike the fear of God in criminals tried in his court of law. He is intelligent and decisive. And her mother's friend as much as her lawyer.

"Will you sign a court order for Dr. Perkins to test Mama's ashes for DNA?" Claire asks. "I have to know if it's really her."

"Let me see what Sheriff Bailey thinks."

"Do we need to involve the police at this stage of the investigation?" Claire asks. "I don't want the public knowing."

He shakes his head. "Everyone will know as soon as the coroner becomes involved. You need to prepare yourself for public opinion to spread like wildfire. To some, Dorothy Powell is notorious." He stows his case files in a drawer and locks it.

"Okay, will you call me as soon as you talk to Bailey?"

"Monday, I'll let you know."

* * *

Claire is maneuvering through Nashville traffic at 5:30 p.m. She doesn't make it home till nearly 6:30. Her daughter's new gray Mazda blocks the driveway. Helen has a key to the backdoor, so Claire presumes she's inside and making herself comfortable.

She unlocks the door and calls out to Helen.

"In here . . ." she stands at the entrance of the hallway, holding her daughter's hand. "Can June stay overnight? Billy's sick, and I don't want her to catch whatever he has."

"Is she contagious, because I don't want to catch what Billy has," Claire says, keeping her distance. "What's wrong with him?"

"He has a stomach virus," Helen replies. "June is not sick. I just picked her up from a birthday party at the park and drove straight over here. Billy's been throwing up all afternoon. Harold took the rest of the day off from work to watch after him."

"Maybe Harold should take Billy to a walk-in clinic," Claire suggests, not in the mood to entertain her granddaughter tonight. She's had a terrible day, and the divorce papers arrived early this morning. This was really happening. Ted is leaving her.

"Mama. Please. I can't deal with two sick children."

"Okay, okay, okay . . ." Claire gives in. "Did you pack enough clothes for the weekend. Billy won't be well for a few days."

"I got everything I need, Granny," the little girl says. "Don't you love me anymore? You don't sound happy I'm here."

Claire looks longingly at June. No way to win today.

9

THE GUYS FRIDAY night poker game will occur at Judge Sewell's prestigious Country Club Estates home on the golf course. He is home by 6:15 p.m. to remove the snacks from the fridge his wife Freida fixed for them earlier today: He carries a platter of sliced apples, pineapple chunks, orange wedges, plus a vine of plump red seedless grapes, down the stairs to his Man Cave. He doubts any of the players will choose fruit over the platters of chicken-salad sandwiches, salty potato chips, and chocolate iced brownies.

Once the food is in place, he unlocks the back patio door. His guests will enter here to avoid the stairs. Freida is paranoid about keeping her light-beige carpet clean, and guys are naturally messy when it comes to shoes. She never complains about him playing poker with his friends as long as he sticks to the rules.

The game is due to begin at seven. Bubba Simpson is the first to arrive. He's the most popular barber in town for business men like himself. Besides, he's been cutting hair for thirty years.

Bubba inherited his business from his father, who inherited it from Bubba's grandfather. His great-grandfather was a founding member of the Columbia Chamber of Commerce and his picture is on the wall of the historic Columbia Courthouse. Bubba isn't the sharpest pair of scissors when it comes to brains, but he knows his cards like the back of his big hands and usually has his fair share of wins. And he is very obese.

"Come on in, Bubba!" James calls out from across the room. "I was just setting out our treats for the evening."

"Hey, Judge. Good to see ya."

"You, too." Bubba requires a wide chair to fit his butt.

Not his real name, but Daryl's Granny had called him Bubba from the time she saw his size after he wiggled out of her daughter's womb. He had weighed eleven pounds at birth, and had been gaining weight ever since. He would top out at 400 lbs.

"Heard you had a late visitor at the office today." Bubba snags a brownie and swallows it whole. "What did Claire Burkes want?" The barber shop is a birthing place for gossip.

The door to the Man Cave opens in time for James to delay his answer. In fact, he has no intention of revealing his conversation with Claire. It is none of Bubba's business.

"Come on in, Peter. I was just getting out the cards. Heard your wife has a bad cold—hope you're not contagious."

"It's just spring allergies. No worries. Hi, Bubba," Peter Dryden glares at the obese man. "If you keep eating Freida's brownies like that, we'll have to carry you back to your car."

"Naw, I know my limits."

"Save one for me," Zane Abel hails from the doorway.

"Freida made me promise you'd eat some of her fruit," James tells the guys. "I said I would, so don't make me into a liar."

They chuckle over the comment. There is one more guest coming, a retired doctor who recently moved to Columbia.

While they wait for Dr. John Bailey to arrive, the guys take turns using the bathroom before finding seats at the large round poker table that accommodates eight players. Only four will play tonight. Six years ago, Arthur Powell, Crawford Perkins, and Clyde Willems had played with the group on Friday evenings.

Unfortunately, all three had been murdered by an assassin hired by a drug cartel run by the Russian Mafia. Town folks were terrified. The door suddenly opens and John Bailey steps inside.

"Sorry, I'm late." John approaches the table. "GPS took me on a wild ride before I found your street, Judge Sewell."

"James, please."

"Welcome, John, glad you could make it," says Zane, James' golf course neighbor. "Hope you came with money to lose."

Everyone laughs, but Zane is not teasing.

John fills the vacant seat at the table. He's a sharper dresser compared to most men who grew up in Columbia. A pediatrician from Atlanta, he'd relocated with his wife Jessica and built a house on the Country Club golf course. Rumor was out, the house cost him more than a million dollars, not counting the double lot.

James deals the cards. Red and blue chips fly on the table as players raise or double. Bubba wins the first round, his smile tucked inside a face so wide it's hardly visible. He's a heart attack waiting to happen. "Thanks, guys. I'll give you a free cut."

"You've already cut a piece out of my wallet," Zane teases.

As the game continues, John has questions about the past murders that had earned front page articles in the Atlanta paper.

"That's all water under the bridge!" James blows off the subject. "Dorothy Powell has moved on with her life."

"Really?" Bubba chuckles. "Not what the grapevine says."

"Who?" Zane asks.

"Kelly Peeler shared some news."

James groans. Impossible to keep a secret in Columbia.

Bubba continues, "Kelly's wife is a nurse at the hospital. As you know, the CSI lab is in the basement. She had lunch with the secretary to Dr. Cynthia Perkin's lab assistant."

"Graham Perkins' wife," Zane makes the connection where he believes Bubba is headed. "What news did she spill?"

"It's all hush and quiet . . ." Bubba leans in to the table. "Somebody's cremated ashes arrived late this morning."

"Whose remains?" Peter blurts out.

"Dorothy Powell's." Bubba proudly sits back.

The guys take a break from cards to discuss Bubba's news further. John Bailey learns enough about the Powell family to write his own book. But he asks few questions, just listens.

* * *

"Tell me a story, Granny," June says as Claire tucks her into bed in the guest bedroom. "A made-up one like GG usually tells me." The little girl's eyelids are drooping.

"I'm not as good at—" Claire almost said lying, "*making up* tall tales like your great-grandmother," she says instead.

"It's okay, do the best you can." June yawns, and pulls the sheet up to her chin. "I love good stories."

Some are too real for Claire, but she doesn't say.

"I'll try June." After they'd eaten a whole microwaved pizza and two caffeine-free cokes, June had still insisted on a bowl of salty popcorn with a Disney movie. It was already eleven p.m.

Claire made up a story about a cat who needed help to find the rat in the house. June fell asleep half way through the tale.

Before closing the door, Claire opens the drawer to the bedside table to retrieve her mother's notebook. She'd been forbidden, even threatened by her mother, if she dared to read what she'd written. But now that she might be . . .

Dead.

Claire reached all the way back in the drawer and found no notebook. It had been right there when she last checked. Soon after her mother had taken a commuter flight out of Columbia.

Did Ted take it when he left?

It bothered Claire that the notes to her mother's proposed book revealing the tricks of the CIA was missing. She'd ask Ted if he took it, and why. But would he tell her the truth?

* * *

It is after midnight. Jessica is still up when John arrives home from his poker game with an elite group of prosperous men who know Columbia like the back of their hands. He cuts out the lights as he walks through the house to the master bedroom.

"You didn't have to wait up for me, Jess."

She puts down the novel she'd been reading in bed and assesses his demeanor. "I wanted to, John."

"That's sweet of you, honey." His shoes are soaked. It was raining cats and dogs by the time the game ended.

"Did you win or lose more often?"

"Lose." He steps out of his pants. "On purpose. I didn't want to be counted out of the next game. "Did the storm wake you?"

"I wasn't sleepy, but the thunder was really loud."

John unbuttons his Polo shirt, then slips out of his slacks that cost more than a poor man's daily pay. "I had a nice time."

"Did you learn anything more about Dorothy Powell?"

"The question is, my beautiful wife, what did you learn from Dorothy's best friend? Is the woman dead or hiding out?"

"I sense that Lorene Perkins doesn't trust me with all her secrets. But Jane and Lizzy appear to be my advocate."

"That doesn't answer my question, Jess." He enters the bathroom to wash his face and brush his teeth. Jess follows and leans on the doorjamb, arms crossed.

"Wh—di—y—think that?" His words are muffled.

"Think what, John?"

"Why Jane and Lizzy are your advocates."

"During the Canasta game, they talked more about Dorothy than Lorene appeared to condone. Facial expressions talk, too."

He grins, toothpaste mixed with saliva dripping in the sink.

"You'll soon fit in, Jess. Don't give up."

"Not if they find out I'm spying on them." Jess sighs. "Can't you let me off the hook? I genuinely like and respect them."

"I hope not enough that you won't help me."

"You mean help your brother!" Jess barks.

"That, too." He'd put that frown on the pretty face.

"I don't want to talk about this anymore." Jess rolls over in the bed, eyes shut tight. She grabs the sheet like it's a life raft.

"Don't be mad at me, Jess. We'll get through this."

10

CLAIRE WAS OVER at the hospital early Monday morning, down at the basement level knocking on the coroner's office door.

"She ain't in yet!" Dr. Gordon Mills hawks—Gordy to his friends if he had any, so Ms. Burke can just butt out.

Claire turns around and faces Cyn's lab assistant.

"What time do you expect her?" she inquires.

"Check the board up front for the week's schedule."

"Nobody dead today that needs to be, uh, evaluated?" Claire hates thinking that her mother had been sectioned and weighed before shoved into an oven so hot it turned her tissues into ashes.

Gordy frowns and simply walks away.

"I should report him," Claire mutters to herself, turning around so fast she bumps into the person she's looking for.

"Claire? It's 6:30 a.m. What are you doing here?"

"I know," her voice comes out as a whisper. "I need to see Mama's ashes." She trails Dr. Cynthia Preston into her office.

"The funeral home will have them if they've arrived."

"Has Lorene spoken to you about examining them?"

"She did, but I can't. Sorry."

"Did Judge Sewell call you yet?" Claire asks.

"This morning? Goodness no, he's probably not even up yet." Cyn thumbs through her voicemail messages.

"Look at me, Dr. Perkins!"

That caught Lorene's daughter-in-law's attention.

"I don't have the ossuary or a court order, Claire."

"I. Am. Not. Leaving. Until I see Mama's ashes."

"Then, go see Blake Johnson. If the package arrived at the post office on Friday, the funeral home should have it."

Cyn continues fiddling with her phone, ignoring Claire.

"Help me, please! I must know if the ashes belong to my mother." Tears materialize. "I won't stop till I'm sure!"

Cyn abandons her desk and walks around it to hug Claire. "Why don't we go to the cafeteria and get some breakfast?"

Claire wilts a bit, thinks about the offer.

"Okay, if you promise to find the ossuary."

"I promise. Come on. It's too early to call the funeral home."

* * *

Lorene Perkins is awake by 8 a.m. Monday morning. As she brews her Maxwell House in the kitchen, she mulls over her last conversation with Jessica Baily on Friday. When their Canasta game ended, Jess had invited her to supper. They had barbeque at Bark's, then they went to see a movie together. Afterwards, Jess wanted ice cream, so they visited a Dairy Queen. Jess asked a ton of questions about Columbia and the murders that occurred some years back. In fact, Lorene realized she'd done most of the talking.

What did she really know about the Baileys? Other than Jess's husband John was a retired doctor, and their daughter in Nashville had died from breast cancer? It felt like Jess was prying.

The subject of Dorothy Powell kept coming up like a revolving door. Why was Jess so interested in Dorothy?

No, I should just keep my mouth shut about Dorothy.

Strangers couldn't be trusted. Just look at the damage Clint Howard caused Dorothy after he moved to town all friendly and smiling? When actually he was Thomas Kessler, a CIA agent up to no good. If Dorothy is alive and Tom is protecting her, then the ashes he's sending to Columbia are a hoax to trick the bad guys.

Is this about the book Dorothy is writing?

While pontificating the issue, the phone rings and Lorene patters over to retrieve her cell from the breakfast bar.

"Yes?" She hears a breathy voice. "Who is this?"

More breathiness.

"Look, if you're stalking me, it isn't worth your trouble. I'm seventy-eight, withering, and I have nothing sexual to offer you."

More breathy sounds.

Then the call ends.

Hmmm, that felt like a threat.

"But, what kind of threat?" she voices.

Lorene punches in the phone number of Jane Murphy.

"What do you want, Lorene?"

"That isn't a very nice way to answer your phone."

"You woke me up. I was having a very sensual dream."

"Shame on you, Jane. That almost sounds pornographic."

"Well, actually it was—so, what do you want?"

"We should meet this morning. I got a call."

"From Claire? Dorothy's ashes are here?"

"No, from nobody."

"That doesn't make sense, Lorene."

"I know, that's why we need to meet. I'll phone Lizzy and we'll let you know where we decide to meet," Lorene concludes.

"You always decide for us. Why not me?" Jane protests.

"Okay, girl, where do you want to meet?"

"Coffee Call on the square. I want one of those delicious pastries with a gourmet cup of foaming coffee." She pauses. "Besides, that's where Dorothy always wants to meet."

"And that's where we usually solved problems together," Lorene says. "To be honest, a sweet latte sounds appealing."

"What time?" Jane asks.

"9:30 at Coffee Call. I'm already hungry."

"I'll see you on the Square."

* * *

After breakfast in the hospital cafeteria, Claire is led by Cyn to a spacious cold-storage room where human remains are stowed in containers and refrigerated. These are marked correctly for expert witnesses to reference as evidence in future court trials. Fresh organs are refrigerated while the ashes of victims killed in fires sit in jars on a shelving unit along one wall.

The scene is surreal. The smells are offensive. Claire had seen enough sickening evidence for a lifetime. "Why are we here?"

Cyn says, "I wanted you to see the amount of evidence I'm required to examine. Each specimen is time dated."

"What you are telling me, Dr. Perkins, is that you don't have time to fool with identifying the mysterious ashes."

"I'm saying it's not my responsibility. I'll speak to both Blake Johnson and Judge Sewell, but I cannot guarantee the outcome."

"Okay, that's fair. I just want someone on my side."

"I understand, Claire, and I am."

"Doesn't it bother you that no one has talked to you about my mama's ashes? You are the forensic expert, after all."

"As far as I know, you're the only one who thinks your mother might not be dead," Cyn points out.

"Lorene does. She was the first to think that."

"Well, ask me, that's assuming quite a lot," Cyn comments.

"I don't know what to do. I don't want to believe my mother is dead. I don't trust Thomas Kessler," Claire admits.

Cyn frowns. "I know you're upset, but you should go home. I'll do what I can to locate the ashes then I'll phone you."

"Is it possible the ashes contain DNA evidence?"

"They don't, Claire," Cyn says with finality.

"Well, that sucks."

"Go home, Claire. I'll phone you when I know more."

* * *

Claire is pissed as she sits in her Buick. She mulls over her conversation with Dr. Perkins before igniting the engine. While driving away from the hospital, she phones Lorene.

"Oh, hi, Claire," she answers.

"Cyn doesn't know anything about Mama's ashes."

"You went to see her without me?"

"I was restless last night. I had to take action," Claire says.

"I knew something fishy is going on," Lorene hails. "The funeral home should have the ossuary by now. We have to figure out why not. The girls and I are getting together at Coffee Call at 9:30 to talk about the strange happenings in Columbia."

"What strange happenings?"

"Jessica Bailey, for one."

"Who is that?" Claire asks.

"A new friend, quite nosy when it comes to Dorothy."

"Will you call me later after you meet with the girls?"

"Why don't you join us for coffee? Maybe you can help us figure out what's going on. Dorothy might be in trouble again."

"She certainly has a talent for that."

"Lorene chuckles. "Spoken by a devoted daughter."

"You think Tom lied in his email to protect Mama?"

"He would if he could. He loves Dorothy," Lorene says.

"Maybe he wants the public to believe she's dead."

"The ashes will tell the truth—if Dorothy's really dead."

"Which leads us back to square one: where are they?"

"Tom has been a terrible influence on Dorothy—using her like a pawn for his own purposes! I hate him!" Lorene exclaims.

"I'm getting there," Claire says.

"I know that's not the way a Christian ought'a think, but he's put Dorothy through the wringer more than once."

"Where are you meeting the girls?" Claire queries.

"Coffee Call on the Square, 9:30."

"See you soon." Claire spins her Buick around in the middle of the street and heads toward the gathering place for business gurus, newcomers, and tourists. News happens at the Columbia Courthouse, the Police Station, or over a social cup of coffee.

11

CLAIRE FOUND A parking space on the square that surrounds the historic Columbia Courthouse where her mother had once been sentenced to a night in jail before she had posted her bail.

She was about to lock up her car and walk to Coffee Call when her cellphone vibrated in her purse. She looked at the caller.

"What is it, Ted?"

"You're still mad," her wandering husband said.

"No, just frustrated. What do you want?"

"Did you read the doc I dropped off on Friday?"

"No, Ted, I've been dealing with my mother's ashes."

"I presume they arrived on Friday."

"No, you presume wrong. They've been misplaced."

He actually chuckles. "That's our Dorothy, playing games."

Claire grits her teeth. "I have an appointment, Ted." It was just coffee, but she was in too foul a mood to deal with him.

"You should have a lawyer go over the divorce papers. It's generous, Claire. You get the house, a monthly stipend, and half my retirement package. I just want to move on with my life."

Claire almost burst into tears.

And leave me behind?

In many ways, divorce is like a death. There is first shock, then anger, then she is about to enter the stage of grieving.

"I will, Ted. Give me a week to respond."

"Okay, Claire. But if you don't . . ."

"Natalie will make you suffer?" she finished his sentence.

"Call me."

The phone went dead.

Claire slams the door to her Buick and pops the locks. She is back to stage two: anger. Grief could wait.

Lorene Perkins, Jane Murphy and Elizabeth Hinson are seated at a table near the back of the vaulted coffee shop that once housed shipping materials for cotton production. During the Civil

War, Nashville had been focal to the battle because of its railway connections between the South and North. Subdivisions had taken root on the outskirts of the city over time, replacing crops like cotton and soybeans. Today, three major interstates crisscross through the city. An hour's drive from the hub of Nashville down I-65, Columbia is a magnet for new businesses and residents.

Lorene waves Claire over.

The sounds of conversations and laughter of the women suddenly lift Claire's wounded spirit. Plus, the delicious odors of pastries loaded in cinnamon and other spices entice the appetite for something decadent. "A latte to die for" will be a temporary remedy to combat her growing anger at Ted for his betrayal.

Claire walks briskly to the table.

"Sorry I'm late," she apologizes.

"No problem, dear," Jane kindly remarks. "We haven't ordered our coffees yet." She slides her menu over to Claire.

"What are you girls having?"

"Undecided," Lizzy chuckles. "Too many choices. I want all the specials. When Lorene asked me to meet, I skipped breakfast. My stomach has been grumbling and moaning for two hours."

Josie their waitress shows up at the table, a pen and order pad in hand. Forget electronic, too technical for her.

"What can I get you girls?"

"I'm having breakfast," Lizzy pipes.

"Me, too," Jane decides.

"The breakfast special is a spinach quiche with fresh fruit on the side." Josie looks at the other two women for a decision.

"I'm having a coffee with a pastry," Claire says.

"Me, too," Lorene says.

"Okay, are we ready to order drinks?" Josie asks.

"Bring us all glasses of water to start with." Lorene takes charge. She wants time to get to the heart of the matter before the food comes. Especially, concerning her talk with Jessica Bailey.

"No, I'm ready to order," Jane says. "I'll take the special, and bring me a vanilla latte." She passes Josie her laminated menu.

"A medium hazelnut latte and an almond pastry," Claire says.

"The breakfast special with an order of those French pastries like they serve in New Orleans," Lizzy orders. "Make sure they're covered in a mountain of powdered sugar." She looks up at Josie. "But first, bring me a caramel latte topped with whipped cream."

Lizzy hands Josie her menu.

"For you, Ms. Lorene?"

"Just a glass of water." So much for a discussion about Jessica Bailey before her friends become indulged in food and coffee.

Lizzy blinks at Lorene. "Are you sick, girl?"

"No, Lizzy, I have never been better."

"Okay, I'll get the waters." Josie hustles off.

"I really like that girl," Jane says. "Her mother works at the library. Josie's a straight A student at Columbia High and plans to attend Vanderbilt on scholarship next fall. Super nice."

"About Jessica Bailey . . ." Lorene launches into the subject she wants to discuss. "I had supper with her on Friday."

"And you're just now telling us?" Jane is surprised.

"Who is Jessica?" Claire asks.

"A newcomer to Columbia," Jane replies. "Jess is super nice. Built a house in the Country Club with her husband John. He's a retired pediatrician from Atlanta, Georgia. When their daughter battled cancer two years ago, they rented a condo in Nashville."

"As I was about to say . . ." Lorene interjects, her voice a decibel higher. "Jess and I had an interesting conversation."

"Why are we discussing Jessica?" Claire inquires.

"Because I'm suspicious of her!" Lorene exclaims.

"Of Jess?" Surprise rests on Jane's wrinkled face. "Why?"

"Oh, don't get me wrong, Claire." Lorene tries to soft-pedal her remarks. "Jess is sweet and kind, personality plus. But she asked me a lot of questions about your mother."

Claire blinks. "Is she my mother's friend?"

"She's never met Dorothy," Lorene replies. "That's why her interest in Dorothy's history in Columbia seems overboard."

"Really!" Lizzy hawks. "Jess is a good person. She's just trying to fit in with us locals. I hope you didn't hurt her feelings."

"What kind of questions did Jess ask?" Claire inquires.

"Do you think Dorothy's really dead? Did she write a book about the CIA? Where do you think she is?" Lorene reveals.

Lizzy says, "Lorene, we all ask ourselves the same questions."

"I know, but why should Jess care? She doesn't know Dorothy." Lorene keeps trying to make her point. "I thought about my conversation with Jess after I got home."

"And what did you conclude?" Claire asks.

"That I did most of the talking and I know nothing about her," Lorene replies. "I think Jess is spying on us."

"Oh, dear . . ." Lizzy frowns. "Why would she?"

"That's my defense for Jess," Jane says.

"How much do we know about her husband John? Why did they move here? And why is Jess asking so many questions?"

"She could be another Clint Howard coming to town!"

"Is that a fair assessment of our new friend?" Jane inquires.

Lorene states, "Thomas Kessler, CIA undercover agent using a false name, moved here. He snooped on all of us. He courted Dorothy so she'd help him with his hidden agenda. I just wonder if John and Jessica have been sent here to snoop again."

"For the CIA?" Claire startles at the idea.

"I think we have to be careful around Jessica Bailey."

12

THE BAILEY'S WERE worn out from their horrendous schedule over the past weekend. Monday morning came too early. As John drinks his coffee at the breakfast bar, trying to wake up, he recalls his busy weekend schedule while Jess stirs up an omelet for them.

Mayor Carson Pierce, Governor Bill Ricardo, Joel Crafton, the Attorney General for the State of Tennessee, and Bubba Simpson had met John for breakfast on Saturday. Soon after ordering, Bubba began pontificating about Columbia's growth, attributes, and financial contribution to the State of Tennessee.

The others at the table endured the obese barber's tirade since he'd heftily contributed to Mayor Pierce's last political campaign. While devouring Charlie Bark's pork breakfast with all the trimmings, John had heard nothing of interest from Bubba.

As Bubba ran out of steam, Judge Sewell began speaking.

"How do you view Dorothy Powell's death?" he asked Governor Bill Ricardo, a second-generation Latino whose wealthy parents moved from South America to Nashville.

"No opinion. First I've heard about that," Bill replies.

"Word's out her ashes are missing," Bubba interjects.

"How did that happen?" The mayor frowns.

"Mix up at the post office," the judge reveals. "First time I heard about it was when Dorothy's daughter nearly assaulted my secretary to get to me on Friday. Claire wants the ashes tested."

"Is there any evidence of tampering?" Joel wonders. He'd driven down to Columbia from Knoxville to meet Carson for breakfast. As fraternity brothers, they'd bonded at the University of Tennessee. Both had gone into politics and stayed friends.

"Always more to the story than meets the eye," Bubba said, adding that Dorothy had single-handedly nearly ruined Columbia's good name by her unorthodox actions. "Might talk to the CIA."

John couldn't believe Bubba had said that.

Coming to the present, he realizes that Jess is leaning over the breakfast bar inches from his face. He blinks, surprised.

"Where did you go, John?"

He clasped her hand. "Just deep in thought. You look lovely this morning, wife. How did you sleep?"

"Pretty well. Afterwards . . ." she grins.

John recalls their tussle in bed last night. He would never find a reason to cheat on Jess. Goodness, he loved this woman.

"Is the coffee made?" he asks.

Jess walks a few steps and grabs a mug from the overhead cabinet. Seconds later, the strong java, no cream, is on the bar.

He sips on the steaming brew. "It's great, Jess."

"You were pretty great yourself last night."

"Don't flatter me, or I may demand more this morning."

"Did you forget you tee off at nine with Judge Sewell?"

He curses then apologizes. "I haven't gotten that far."

Jess laughs. "I did upset your apple cart last night."

A silly grin spreads over John's face. "You really did."

"How did your breakfast with Mayor Pierce go on Saturday?"

"Fine. Anything new about Dorothy come up at your Canasta game on Friday?" He flips through the morning *Gazette*.

"After the game, I had supper with Lorene Perkins."

"Really! And you're just telling me *this* now?"

"We both were busy over the weekend." Jess had spent Saturday morning at the beauty shop getting her hair done, then played a round of tennis at the Club with a new neighbor.

"Are you going to tell me if you learned anything knew about Dorothy during supper?" John glares.

"Let me just say one thing on the subject, John: I don't like snooping on my friends. For me, it's been a real struggle."

"Aw, Jess. . . you still have good friends in Atlanta."

She sighs. "It appears out of sight is out of mind."

The conversation feels strained, and that bothers Jess.

"What about your tennis partner, Sheila Golson?"

"She divorced a year ago and moved."

"So, she doesn't have our new address," John concludes. "I'm sorry you're lonely, Jess. I thought moving to a new location and building a house would help both of us get over Rita's death."

Jess's eyes blaze with anger.

"I'll never get over our daughter's death, John."

"Come here." He rounds the bar and hugs Jess. "I'm sorry I was so harsh. Forget what I just said, I'm such a fool."

Tears in her eyes, Jess gazes into John's eyes, so green they stand out like jewels against his tan face. He's sixty-six years old and wears his physique well. He's fit from regular gym workouts and daily golf games. There's not an ounce of fat on his torso.

"No, John, I'm sorry, too. I take full responsibility for my loneliness and lack of true friends. I'm going to work on that."

"So, I'm forgiven?" He holds Jess at arm's length.

"Yes, but one more thing . . ."

"Okay, I'm listening." He focuses on her pretty face.

"Is it fair to us for you to spy on Dorothy Powell's friends for your brother? We don't work for the damn government, John. Let Joshua do his own spying. It's *his* job, not ours."

"He needs my help, Jess."

"And you never say no to him." She nods.

"We'll finish all this snooping before long, Jess."

"If death doesn't finish us first."

John laughs. "You're overthinking the problem, honey!"

"It's not funny, John. Your brother plays for keeps." Jess shakes her head. "Besides, I enjoy playing cards with Dorothy's friends. They've made me feel welcome here. Don't ruin that."

"Really, Jess, I'm sorry you're struggling. Let's see what we can find out about Dorothy for Josh, then we'll quit. Okay?"

"Promise?"

"Yes." He kisses her lightly.

Her eyes roll in thought.

"Another thought on the subject?"

"No. I just want to thank you for agreeing to attend the Methodist church with me next Sunday. Maybe we'll meet some decent couples that have something in common with us."

"You mean those without political baggage?"

"Don't read so much in what I say, it's annoying."

"I guess I'm more like my brother than I'd like to think," John confesses. "I love you and I care what you think."

"I guess I'm wearing my feelings on my sleeves today."

"Hey, don't put yourself down, Jess. It pleases me to know you're settling in and making new friends."

"Thank you, John. I know you enjoy getting together with the Friday-night poker club, but this is our retirement time. We need to concentrate more on our needs as a couple. I want to make some travel plans. See more of this beautiful world. I want to poke my toe in the Nile River in Egypt. I want—"

"Stop, Jess. Be patient, dear. All in good time . . ."

"I'm tired of pretending to be a friend, John. I want to be honest and real with the people I meet. Can you understand that?"

"I can, sweetheart. Everything is so new. Help me help Josh and we'll end this soon. I'll do my part and you do yours."

Jess looks at her husband.

Did he hear anything I said?

13

TUESDAY MORNING, GEORGE Taylor is in the mail room of the Columbia Post Office, puzzled over why the Post Master had directed him to replace a label on a parcel that arrived a week ago on Friday from Belize in Central America. As instructed, he had mailed the parcel to another address, a post-office box in Langley, Virginia. To add to his angst, Beryl had told him not to mention the task. George had worked in this same position at the post office for the past twenty-three years. He was worried that someone would find out. Tampering with mail is a federal crime.

Yet, Beryl was insistent that he had received the authority to redirect the package to a different address. No details had been shared with George, but he knew the CIA headquarters were located in Virginia. The idea of committing a crime is troubling.

* * *

As John suggested, Jess phones Lorene Perkins on Tuesday. She was feeling better about spying since it was short-lived.

"Hi, this is Jessica Bailey," she begins the conversation. "I really enjoyed our time together this past Friday. I told John how much I enjoy playing cards, and how nice you girls were to me. He wants to meet all of you in person." She stops talking.

"Really?"

"Yes, my husband is a wonderful host."

"Okay, Jess. What do you have in mind?"

"A cookout at our house this Friday. Right after we finish playing cards. I'd like the cell numbers for Jane and Lizzy."

"Sure. I'll text you their numbers. Supper sounds like fun."

What a great opportunity to learn more about the Baileys.

"Well, then, I'll see you at the Canasta table on Friday."

"It's a date, Jess."

* * *

When the call ends, Lorene delays texting Jess with Lizzy's and Jane's phone numbers. She should get their permission first.

Lizzy answers on the first ring.

"Were you sitting on your phone waiting for me to call?"

"Don't be cute, Lorene, I have a headache."

"Well, I didn't give it to you."

"Did you have a reason for calling?"

"Jessica Bailey has invited us for supper on Friday. She says it is John's idea," Lorene explains. "I said we'd come."

"Without first talking to me and Jane?"

"Look, Lizzy, this is an opportunity. We'll find out a lot about how the Bailey's live and what they think about Columbia."

"And why Jess asks so many questions about Dorothy?"

"Of course! Why else would we accept their invitation?"

"You still don't trust Jess," Lizzy says.

"Trust must be earned, haven't you heard?"

"Okay, I'm on board."

"Okay, take two Tylenol. I need to call Jane now."

"Yes, Dr. Lorene. Goodbye."

That call ends, so Lorene phones Jane. She's ecstatic over the invitation. She wants to know what to wear.

"Casual, we're going over to the Bailey's house as soon as our Canasta game ends on Friday," Lorene says.

"Jess is just the nicest person," Jane pontificates. "I can't imagine she has any reason to spy on us. Do you?"

"That's for us to find out, Jane."

"Well, you can count on me."

"Great!" Lorene exclaims. "Dorothy will be proud of you."

"Yes, if she is still breathing."

"Don't doubt it, Jane," Lorene says. "We'll get into Jess's head and find out more about John. Fool us once, not twice."

"You're thinking of Clint Howard," Jane reasons.

"We can't readily trust newcomers until we've vetted them, Jane. Trust must be earned," Lorene passionately states.

"I get it. I'm all in. Bring on the party!"

"And don't forget what we talked about at Coffee Call."

"Remind me." They'd discussed a lot of subjects.

"No mention of Claire's divorce. Don't bring up Dorothy. Listen and don't run your tongue so much, and—"

"I get it, Lorene. I'm on board," Jane says.

"Good. The Bailey's don't need to know everything we know. It's none of their Double D-D business!"

"You sound just like Dorothy!" Jane chuckles.

"Thank you for the compliment, friend."

"Poor Claire. I've never seen her so upset. Imagine losing both a mother and a husband at the same time."

"I know . . ." Lorene sniffles, "I almost peed in my pants when Claire told us she'd received the divorce papers on Friday. If someone as nice and pretty as Claire can't hold onto a guy, our young granddaughters do not have a chance in Hell."

"I think you meant, a prayer in heaven," Jane says. "Let's don't give the devil any power over our granddaughters."

"Sorry, slip of the tongue."

"Well, let's hope the next generation has more faith in people than we do!" Jane voices. "I'll keep my lips zipped about Claire, but I won't lie if I'm asked a question. It's not Christian."

"Neither is murder, Jane. Get your priorities straight."

"Just so we're clear on the party rules."

"Okay, okay . . . just keep any information about Dorothy vague, okay? Let me take the lead if you hit a snag. Jess is smart. I don't know John yet, so we should not underestimate him. We are humble people, Jane, far from understanding how deceit works."

"Did you caution Lizzy like you have me?" Jane asks.

"I don't play favorites with my best friends."

"Just checking," Jane mutters.

"Now, I need to strategize how we can get the Bailey's to talk about themselves," Lorene says. "We need to be prepared before we three stooges walk into a spy trap set by Dr. John Bailey."

"Okay, I need to clean my house and pick up a blouse at the cleaners," Jane utters. "See you on Friday."

"Wait! Your blouse is not washable?" Lorene asks. "It costs a fortune to have clothes professionally cleaned these days."

"No choice. I spilt coffee down my new green silk blouse at church on Sunday. I tried spot-cleaning it, but . . ."

"Okay, then, it's your pocketbook."

* * *

John had been standing behind Jess as she talked to Lorene Perkins. When the call ended, he asks, "Are they coming?"

Jess turns around and frowns.

"Were you eavesdropping on my conversation?"

"Yeah, Jess, but you handled Lorene beautifully."

"Just hearing your compliment sets my nerves on edge. I feel like a heel inviting my three newest friends over for supper so you can grill them and ask questions your brother won't."

"Talking about Joshua, he phoned me before you got up this morning. I'm meeting him in Atlanta on Thursday."

"Why?" Jess snaps. "Doesn't he have important work to do?"

"Calm down, baby. We're doing a good thing for America."

"You think?" Jess shakes her head. "Lying and spying."

"We're just entertaining Dorothy's friends. Don't go paranoid on me, honey. You may not trust Josh, but trust me. Okay?"

"I'm not so sure your motives are pure, either. I need you home to help with the cookout on Friday."

"Of course, I'll help. We'll burn burgers on the grill. I'll order slaw and baked beans from Kroger and have the food delivered Friday afternoon. Dorothy's friends aren't high society."

"Ha! They have no idea what trouble they're getting into."

"Don't think like that, Jess. Just try to have a good time."

"You will be back from Atlanta before five on Friday?"

"I promise." He kisses her on the forehead.

"You better, Johnny-boy, or you're in big trouble."

He laughs. "I like your kind of trouble, Jess. I know how to be nice to our guests. Go ahead and hire a cleaning service to tidy up the mess on Saturday morning. We'll enjoy a nice meal, good conversation, and hopefully learn something new about Dorothy."

"I like the sound of that, John."

"When the party's over, and our guests have gone, we'll cozy up in the patio swing and watch the full moon set late."

"And if it should rain?" Jess worries their lives are skidding out of control—just like the time Rita contracted cancer.

"If it rains, honey, we'll invent our own moon."

* * *

Claire is at home in Brentwood, making a late lunch on Tuesday. Ted's divorce papers are scattered out on the breakfast bar. She's reread his generous offer three times, but is still not comfortable signing on the dotted line. It feels so final.

He is offering her $10,000 a month alimony and half his retirement package. On the surface, it's fair. What concerns her most is the contract's future impact on her children—how his assets will be divided between his son with Natalie and their children. She doesn't want Helen and Patrick slighted.

She has an appointment with an attorney early this afternoon to discuss the settlement offer. Regardless of what she decides, Ted should be punished for his betrayal. After a successful forty-year marriage, he'd cheated on her with a woman nearly half his age. No doubt, Natalie initiated the affair since Ted was prime for the taking. A wealthy, middle-aged man unhappy at home.

She recognizes that an influential attorney would provide a better living situation with all the amenities she alone cannot afford. Ted will be a devoted, loving father who will teach their son all he needs to know to survive in a dog-eat-dog society.

At those thoughts, Claire cries tears into her plate.

14

WEDNESDAY CAME ROARING in like a lion with wind, lighting, thunder, and hard rain. George Taylor had taken the day off, reporting he was coming down with a cold. Moody and nervous. The real reason he didn't want to work is because of what took place Friday a week ago. His coffee cup had shattered when he dropped it. His wife Shelly cleaned up the mess a bit worried.

"George. You should see a doctor."

He mews from the recliner, his bare feet elevated. "I don't need no doctor, honey. My condition is more mental."

Shelly dumps the broken glass in the garbage can, walks over to the recliner, and feels George's head.

"Your brow is cold, so you don't have a temp." She shakes her head. "Are you getting Alzheimer's?"

"Hell, no, Shelly! Leave me alone. I just need to think."

"Well . . . I have some house cleaning to do this morning. Keep hydrated and try to rest. For goodness sakes, don't take whatever's bothering you out on me. I'm on your side."

George plops his feet on the den floor carpet and sits up straight. "I think I committed a crime, Shelly."

"When? Did you rob an ATM?"

"Worse. I repackaged a parcel from Belize and sent it to an address in Langley, Virginia," he reveals.

"Where is Belize?"

"In Central America. The parcel was supposed to be delivered to Johnson's Funeral Home."

"It was a body?" Shelly startles.

"More like ashes in an urn," he replies. "Beryl told me to do it and not to ask questions. Don't tell anyone, he said."

George scrubs his matted eyes, then looks at his wife.

"You said Langley, Virginia. Did you send the body to the CIA complex?" She worries George will lose his job.

"No, a post-office box number."

"I admit that sounds clandestine."

He nods. "Yeah, it does."

"So, George, you disobeyed your boss and told me?"

"I can't bear sitting on this secret anymore."

"Well, I'm glad you told me, George. I think your only crime is doing what Beryl asked you to do. He committed the crime."

"Anyhow, I'm thinking of talking to a lawyer about it."

"Is there anything else you need to tell me?"

"On Monday, Dr. Cynthia Perkins called Blake at the funeral home and asked him to deliver the parcel to the lab."

"How do you know?"

"I got my hair cut. Bubba told me."

"Why is the coroner interested in the parcel?"

"That's my question." He glares at Shelly. "Of course, Blake told Dr. Perkins he didn't receive the package on Friday."

"Do you have any idea what was inside?" Shelly reacts.

"It's rumored an urn with Dorothy Powell's ashes."

"She's dead? By natural causes?" More questions surface.

"I don't know. What if she was murdered?"

"Then those ashes are a hot item," Shelly concludes.

"Honey, I don't want to lose my pension from doing something illegal, even if the Post Master told me to do it."

Shelly mulls over his dilemma.

"You should be concerned, George, but talk to Beryl first and get the facts. If the CIA requested the parcel, it must be legal."

"Don't count on it, Shelly."

* * *

"Why are you packing to leave for Atlanta today, John?"

"I can't play golf today when it's raining." He tosses an extra pair of socks in his suitcase. "Josh is expecting me."

"Remember you promised to help with the cookout on Friday for the girls," Jess says. "Elderly" sounds so old.

"I'll keep my promise. Before I leave this morning, I'll order the food from Kroger. Don't worry about anything but having a nice time with your new Canasta friends. Hopefully, we can learn something more valuable about Dorothy Powell's jaded life."

He candidly rocks his head then grins.

"What, John?"

"Her friends are hiding something."

Jess parks hands on her hips. "Everyone is not deceitful, John. What's happened to you? Don't you trust anybody?"

"I trust you, Jess."

"Well, ask me, your brother's MO is rubbing off on you."

John glances up after tying his tennis shoes. "Talk about trust, Jess. You're no sweetheart to my brother when he visits."

"Hard to be civil when I despise him."

"Are we about to argue over my task?"

"No, let's don't fuss, John. This is our retirement. I want us to get back to what we used to have—trust and love. I was so lonely when you worked non-stop at the pediatrician office. It felt like I was single most of the time. I want to feel cherished."

John hefts his lean muscular frame off the bed and walks over to Jess. "I do love you, honey. But Josh is my brother. I've never cheated on you with another woman. It was just work."

"The only affair you are having now is with your brother!" Jess lashes out. "I think he's more important to you than I am!"

* * *

John arrives in Atlanta, Georgia by 2 p.m. He finds his brother at the gym working out. "Donna told me you were here."

Donna is Joshua's significant other. They live together.

"Thanks for coming early, John. I have some information you need to see that pertains to your assignment in Tennessee."

John hawks, "I'm not working for the damn CIA, Josh. I'm simply doing you a favor, so let's cut the crap and get on with it."

"Okay, let me grab a shower and we'll head back to the apartment." He lives near the airport for convenience.

"Sure, I'll wait up front."

Donna has a delicious dinner prepared that evening. It had stormed all day in Atlanta, so there wasn't much to do but share a bit about their separate lives and watch some television. When Donna went to bed at nine, Josh wanted to get into the details of his probing into Dorothy Powell's past. First, John had a question.

"Are you going to marry Donna?"

"Is that any of your business?"

Josh was near retirement age for a federal agent but had never sustained a long-term relationship due to his periodic absences in carrying out the CIA's undercover assignments. He'd worked all over the Middle East during the 1990s when terrorism had reared its ugly head and threatened Americans. But John had hopes that this union with Donna might actually work out.

"She is good for you," John defends his question.

"Okay, okay . . ." Josh throws a hand. "You're just looking out for me. You think I'll retire and become a lonely old man."

Josh hasn't told John, but he's planning to retire from the CIA in two years, as soon as he finishes this last assignment.

"Follow me. I want to show you something."

He leads the way down the hall to his office, usually kept locked when he was not working. Donna doesn't know about his secretive life. She thinks he's a business man. She's a good moral person, and he has to do bad things sometimes. In fact, he could be labeled schizophrenic when it comes to separating his work life from personal ties. He unlocks the door and they go inside.

"Why am I here, Joshua?" John queries as the door closes.

"I want you to see this file I recently received from Langley. It's a full report on Dorothy Powell's escapades over the past six years." He opens facing John. "Take a careful read, Bro."

John sits in the chair and opens the folder. He's a fast reader, but there's a lot of information. When he finishes, he looks up.

"So, CIA Agent Thomas Kessler spied on Dorothy first, posing as the Director for the Columbia Senior Citizen Center. He romanced her, gained her trust, then coerced her to steal millions of dollars from international banks?" Un-be-liv-able!

"Yeah, he took advantage after her husband was murdered."

"How?"

"A Russian assassin was sent," Josh replies.

"Why?"

"Dorothy is the spitting image of Tom's first wife."

"Was? She's dead."

"Also murdered over thirty years before Tom suckered Dorothy. Angela Kessler was a double-agent who worked for both the CIA and Russia's SVR. She set up the bank accounts and deposited stolen funds in the early 1990s," Josh reveals. "With a little trickery, Dorothy fooled everyone and withdrew the funds."

"Who is this woman? I thought she was a farmer's wife."

"When Arthur Powell was found dead on the banks of Crystal Creek, his death was first viewed as an accident."

"I sense a big *but* . . ." John says.

"Except the assassin planted evidence in Arthur's workshop that convinced a detective that Dorothy murdered him for the life-insurance policy payout," Josh says. "Half a million."

"And we both know that money talks." John chuckles.

"Dorothy is a retired school teacher, smart and attractive for her age. She never accepted that Arthur fell off his tractor and struck his head on a rock. She caused a big stir in Columbia."

"Why is she important to the CIA now?"

"She's writing a book about them," Josh reveals.

"Wow, who would've thought?" John whistles.

"The CIA won't let her tell their secrets. So, I'm spying on Dorothy's friends," Josh says. "And I need your help."

"For what purpose, if she's dead?"

"The CIA believes Dorothy is hiding somewhere safe, so she can finish her book. Plus, she needs a reliable publisher."

John whistles. "CIA secrets revealed will be a best-seller."

"Question: Is Thomas Kessler helping Dorothy?"

15

THE CANASTA GAME ended at 4:30 p.m. on Friday. Between potty breaks, Jess had phoned John's cell and gotten his voicemail. He wasn't home when she'd left at 1:30 and that pissed her off.

But, to John's credit, the food had arrived at 1:15 p.m.

She was a little late for the game, but the girls were socially engaged with friends. The buzz was that a mysterious package had arrived at the post office last Friday and was redirected to Langley, Virginia. Shelly Taylor's husband George worked at the post office and had told her about it. She'd shared the news with a friend, who told another friend, until Lizzy Perkins had overhead the secretive conversation between Bubba's wife and the mayor's wife. No secrets stay hidden for very long in Columbia.

The grapevine was far faster than the internet.

"We know what was in that package," Lorene whispers to Jane as they sit at the table on the outside patio of the Senior Citizen Center. Lizzy is still talking to Bubba's wife.

"Sorry I'm late, girls, but I had to deal with our food delivery." Jane sets her large purse on the floor by her chair at the table. "Did I miss something important?"

"No," Lorene quickly replies, "just some local gossip."

"Food for *our* supper?" Lizzy comments on the delivery.

"Yes, John ordered baked beans and slaw from Kroger. I already have prime beef patties ready to go on the grill. All of the vegetable trimmings are in the fridge. We won't go away hungry."

Lorene hawks, "As if that's possible."

"We're all spreading in the middle." Jane groans as she deals the first round of cards. Everyone studies their hand of 13 cards.

Lizzy is Lorene's partner and plays first. She has only one red three, grateful she doesn't need to worry about the other team scoring four reds and earning 800 points at the end of the game.

"What gossip did I miss?" Jess grabs a breath.

"Just some juicy news going around," Lorene vaguely replies, her worried gaze chasing after Lizzy. *Don't tell her anything!*

"Something interesting I should know about?" Jess locks eyes with Jane Murphy. "Don't keep secrets from me, girls. Columbia is my home, now that I have set down permanent roots!"

Lorene hawks, "The gossip is not worth sharing. It's a rumor that no one should have started in the first place."

Jess sits back. "Okay, then why do I feel like you're keeping something from me, Lorene? Is this gossip about me or John?"

Lizzy appears perplexed. "No, dear! No! We'd never!"

"It's just that we like to keep our secrets close to the vest," Lorene explains. "We really don't know you all that well."

"That's really mean!" Jane snaps at Lorene. "Jess doesn't deserve to be treated like a stranger! Apologize to her. Now!"

"Okay, okay . . ." Lorene waves a hand, "I apologize. I'm just wearing my feelings on my shoulders today." A tear drips from one cheek. "I guess you've heard rumors about Dorothy Powell."

"We're all sad she's not here with us," Jane adds.

"So, this is gossip you're not sharing?" Jess frowns. "Is it related to Dorothy's recent death?"

"We're not sure," Lorene tentatively replies.

Lizzy protests, "This is ridiculous, Lorene! We need to tell Jess what's circling through the gossip grapevine."

"That's so sweet, Lizzy, to be included." Jess smiles.

Lorene grits her teeth and proclaims, "You haven't met Shelly Taylor. Her husband George works for the post office."

"So . . .?" Jess waits for the news to drop.

"So, apparently he received a mysterious package from Belize in Central America last Friday, and it was rerouted to a post-office box in Langley, Virginia," Lorene reveals.

"Why is that important?" Jess inquires.

"We believe the parcel contains Dorothy's ashes."

"Really?" Jess exclaims. "Who was the recipient?"

"Of the package?" Lizzy tries to track Jess's thought.

"We were told by a friend that Dorothy's ashes would be sent to Johnson's Funeral Home, but the urn never arrived. We think that package was sent to the CIA headquarters," Lorene explains.

"Yes, but we can't report it to the authorities," Lizzy says. "We don't want to get Shelly's husband George fired. The Post Master specifically told him not to tell a soul."

"But George told his wife," Jess concludes.

"And she told a friend," Lizzy adds.

"And that friend told another friend," Jane says.

"And he told his barber, Bubba Cross," Lizzy declares.

"And Bubba told everyone that came into his shop yesterday. The package is the buzz of Columbia. We all want to know what that's about." Jane looks at Lorene. "Do you have a comment?"

"No, I think you've both said it all."

* * *

The girls drove their own cars to Jess's house on the Country Club Golf Course. Rain had enriched the spring greenery at the entrance and made everything look and smell fresh. Rows of colorful plants lined the sidewalk to Jess's red-brick one-story house that stretched endlessly over an acre lot.

Jess lifts the garage doors with a fob. Relieved, she spies John's car parked there. He is home from Atlanta. She waits for the girls on the front porch. John opens the front door, grinning.

"Come on in, girls! Welcome to our humble abode."

"Is this some joke?" Lizzy whispers to Jane.

Jess looks hard at John. Something seems off with him, the way he stands; the way he looks at her like he could eat her up. They'd just had good sex before he left, so what's up with him?

"Come inside and get comfortable!" Jess hails.

Lorene, Jane, and Lizzy enter the vaulted foyer and glance around. The floor beneath their feet is paved in white stone. They follow Jess into a spacious den with a fireplace large enough for the Wicked Witch to cook Hansel and Gretal over its flames.

Jane recalls how children loved reading that gory storybook.

"What can I get you girls to drink?" John flashes a witty smile. "We have bottled water and sodas. For those daring, I have red or white wine. For the really bad girls, I have whisky."

Jess blinks back surprise.

John chuckles. "I can even mix you a margarita."

Who is this man I'm married to?

"We don't drink alcohol," Lorene declines. "We all go to church. I'm a Baptist and it's against my principles."

John frowns. "How 'bout at soda then?"

"Bottled water, thank you." Lorene instinctively doesn't trust this man, even if he is Jess's husband. He has mean green eyes.

"Well, girls, why don't we go outside while John gets our beverages." She opens the double-sliding doors to the patio.

Lorene plops down on the glider and stares at the pristine golf green. The sun magnificently dips, spreading color across the western horizon. As the day closes, a cool breeze stirs.

"This is comfy, Jess," Jane says as she sits in a chair.

"John's an avid golfer. We both enjoy the view."

"You truly have a lovely property," Lizzy says, sitting at the round glass-top table. "I still don't understand why you'd move to Columbia when Atlanta has so much to offer in social activities."

"It was John's choice."

"That's a surprise," Lorene says. "Why?"

"He retired and is tired of the Atlanta traffic."

"I think you made a good choice," Jane interjects. "Our town has a country atmosphere, but we're close enough to Nashville if you like music. Oh, the city is always sponsoring concerts."

"When our daughter got sick last year, we wanted to live closer to her. We rented a condo in Nashville before deciding to build here. After Rita passed, we decided to stay," Jess explains. "Both John and I love Middle Tennessee's rolling hillsides."

"We love it, too," Jane says. "I'm a fourth-generation resident. My greats from way back settled in Maury County."

"We all have our reasons for moving here," John says as he comes out on the patio holding a large tray with their beverages.

"Here, I'll help you, John," Jess says.

"Thanks, love, but I got it."

Jess sits back down.

"Okay, girls, I have a Coke, a Pepsi, a Sprite, and two waters." He grins. "You pick." He holds the tray for them to choose.

"Jess said you took a quick trip to Atlanta," Lorene starts the conversation. "Do you still have business there?"

"Nope. My brother lives there. We like to meet."

"That's nice," Jane says. "My brother passed when he was sixty. Two months before that, my father died. Then my mom."

John frowns. "Life can sure be a bitter pill."

"It sure can," Lizzy says, then gives her version of putting death to bed. By the time she finishes, everyone is depressed.

"Let's talk about something joyful!" Lorene pipes.

"I'm hungry, John. Maybe you should start the burgers." Jess feels as if her visitors are not having the good time she'd hoped.

16

FRIDAY EVENING, CLAIRE is seated on the sofa in the den. Ted had arrived at the house ten minutes before. He slouches in the wingback, shoulders bent like he's aged ten years since she'd seen him. His coming this late in the day isn't a good sign.

"What do you want, Theodore?"

"Just came by to thank you for accepting my offer and signing the divorce papers. If I can do anything else . . ."

"For me? Hell no, Ted! Please! You've done quite enough."

If Claire could stare any harder, he would be on the floor.

"I know this isn't easy for you," he says.

"Apparently, it's not all that easy on you, either, Ted. Considering the way you look. But, that's none of my business anymore. You've broken ties and so I bid you good luck."

"Well, it was kind of you not to contest the divorce. We both know fighting in court will hurt our children," he offers.

"They're already hurt, Ted, since you've abandoned us."

"No, I have not abandoned Helen or Patrick. They can ask for my help at any time." Ted is doing his best to peacefully part with Claire. He doesn't want to cause any more harm.

"No problem, Ted. When trash needs to be taken out, I never hesitate." She actually grins. "Now go, Lover Boy, and enjoy the rest of your life. I hope your new wife leaves you for a younger man—and takes as much of your money with her as she can."

"Clllaaaiiirrr . . ."

"Be careful you don't choke on my name, Theodore. It would be a terrible shame if you dropped dead in my house." Her arms are crossed. "Somebody might accuse me of murder."

Ted's hazel eyes limp from fatigue. "I didn't mean for any of this to happen, Claire. You can't plan on how love plays out." He grabs the wingback's sidearms to maintain his balance.

"I know, and I truly empathize, Ted." Claire's Robin-blue eyes widen with amusement. "I know you intended to keep your sordid affair with Natalie a secret. You wanted to enjoy a tangle in the sheets with her, then come home to me every night for a nice home-cooked meal and good night's rest."

Ted straightens his bowed body. "You don't have to be so mean about our parting. What will Helen think?"

Claire laughs. "My, my, Ted. Do you really believe that Helen still respects you? And, to be honest, when did you ever find the time from your busy schedule to play ball with Patrick? Our children are grown and really don't care that much about you."

"You're bitter, Claire." Ted represses anger. "I should go."

"Most sensible thing you've said since you walked through my door." Claire points at it. "Show your way out, I'll lock up."

"Goodbye, Claire, you have my cell number."

"No, I've actually deleted it," she huffs.

As Ted heads for the door, Claire grabs the folder with the divorce papers and calls out, "Don't forget your ticket out of my life, Ted! And remember, this wrecked train only leaves."

The slamming door still startles Claire. She waits a second to take in what just happened. Then she bursts into tears.

* * *

Back at the Bailey's house on the Country Club Golf Course, the Canasta girls are lounging on the patio, drinking their sodas.

Suspecting John had been nipping on the liquor while in the kitchen, Jess tells him she'll take care of the drink orders while he gets their burgers going on the grill. Something about him is off.

While John labors over the grill, the girls talk about the pretty weather while watching the sun recede behind clouds puddled in color. The cooler breeze is refreshing mixed with floral odors.

"This is truly nice, Jess," Jane hails from her chair. "I'm really glad we connected with you at the Center." She refers to the Senior Citizen Center where many retirees gather to socialize.

"I'm glad, too, Jane. If I hadn't dropped my sack of groceries in Kroger last month, and you hadn't stopped to help me, we might never have met. I'm grateful for your friendship."

I bet you are. Lorene is not so sure the newcomer to Columbia is telling the truth. There are baskets for groceries at Kroger. You don't have to carry a big paper sack yourself to the car. There are employees to help you with that. *No, something smells fishy.*

"I really hope you get to meet Dorothy," Lizzy tells Jess. "You would really like her. She's smart and sassy—just like you. And she dresses like a million-dollar baby."

"I heard she collected insurance on her deceased husband after he died," Jess says. "Was it a great deal of money?"

"Five-hundred thousand dollars!" Jane exclaims. "Probably not a lot for you, but for most of us locals, it is."

"Really, Jane?" Lorene eyeballs her, unhappy that Dorothy's life has been brought up for discussion again.

"Did I miss anything, girls?" John stands in the open doorway to the patio holding a pan of raw burger patties. "Grill's hot now, so here goes. Fifteen minutes and we all pig out."

Jess abandons her chair. "I'll bring out the fixings. Jane? Will you help me carry out the potato salad, baked beans, and slaw?"

"Of course." The prim retired librarian hustles out the door.

John flattens the burgers on the grill and they sizzle and smoke. "Were you girls talking about Dorothy Powell?"

"What if we were?" Lorene speaks before thinking.

"Last Friday at Judge Sewell's house, over a game of Poker, her name came up. Evidently, she's pretty famous around here."

"Oh, she certainly is!" Lizzy brags. "Single-handedly, Dorothy took down an assassin that killed her Arthur."

Lorene's lemony eyes bug out at Lizzy.

John whistles and pats the burgers with a spatula. "She sounds like a brave woman. I hear she was once abducted by a CIA agent." He stands loosely, looking like a movie star.

Lorene shakes her head at Lizzy. *Shut up, girl!*

"Oh, yes. Thomas Kessler. He's a piece of work. Wooed and screwed her—" Lizzy stops, embarrassed. "Well, not literally."

"Dorothy was a good Methodist," Lorene defends her honor.

"*Was?* Past tense? You believe she's dead?"

"I don't know, John," Lorene replies. "I do know Dorothy doesn't sleep around. On the other hand, we don't know much about you or Jess. Enlighten us, please."

He flips the burgers. "My past is pretty boring in comparison to Dorothy Powell's." The look in his eyes is playful.

"Then you'll fit right in with most of us," Jane interjects.

"Okay, Lorene, what do you want to know?"

"Let's start easy, shall we? Why did you choose Columbia?" She will change the subject from Dorothy's past or die trying.

"Oh, that's easy! We love Tennessee. It's got all the seasonal changes Georgia has, plus Nashville is the entertainment center of the world. What's not to like about Columbia? Friendly people. Good churches. Couldn't find a better place to hang your hat."

Huh, his answer seems a bit overboard!

"And Jess likes the rolling green hills," Lizzy adds.

"We both do." John flips the burgers. "Something was mentioned about a lost package at the Post Office," he pursues his inquiry. "Know anything about that, Lorene?"

"Me? I don't.!" She shakes her head.

"Me, either," Lizzy adds, taking Lorene's cue.

"Anything about what?" Jess brings out a large platter with sliced pickles, tomatoes, and green lettuce. Jane sets the potato salad, beans, and slaw on the table next to the salad fixings.

"The missing urn with Dorothy's ashes," Lizzy pipes.

Lorene slaps Lizzy's arm. "Got that mosquito!"

Ouch! Shocked, Lizzy rubs her arm.

"So . . . back to the topic of Dorothy," John revisits the interesting subject. "Do you have any idea where she is?"

"What do you mean?" Jane's gaze skitters to Lorene.

"Her ashes, of course." John's lips wiggle.

Lorene can't tell if it's a frown or a mean grin.

"I don't think anyone knows, John," Jess intervenes, tired of the interrogation of her friends. "Are the burgers done?"

John carefully lays the meat on heated buns with melted cheese and divvies them out on plates. "*Bon appetit!*"

Lorene has to admit the food is fantastic. Everyone ate too much, forgetting about calories. John kept prying, but Jess did a good job diverting the conversation back to their Canasta game.

The Bailey's guests left the house around 8:30 p.m. She was tired, but John appeared energetic. He was fit for a marathon.

They cleaned away the supper clutter and turned the lights out in the kitchen and den. Jess was undressing in the master bedroom when she caught John ogling her.

"What's up with you, John? You're different since you got home from Atlanta. Did your evil twin rub off on you?"

He scoffs, "I don't know why you don't like Joshua. He's a good guy underneath that façade of toughness."

She removes her shirt and bra and glares at him.

"Why are you staring? You've seen me naked before."

"No, no, continue, please, I'm loving this show."

Jess walks into the bathroom and slams the door. Something is up with John. She shakes her head. Is he having an affair?

17

EARLY SATURDAY, CLAIRE receives a second email from Thomas Kessler. Attached is a document with specific instructions for her mother's memorial service. Where she wants the service to be held and how the ashes are to be scattered.

Is this Tom's idea of a sick joke?

Claire is so upset she phones her daughter Helen.

"Mama, it's 2 a.m. Shouldn't you be sleeping?"

"I can't, Helen. I got another disturbing email from Tom Kessler. He sent Mama's instructions for her memorial service."

"I didn't know Grammy wrote anything about that," Helen expresses surprise. "She expected to outlive us all. Only the rapture of Jesus Christ could convince her to leave this world."

"I know, I know . . . so this doesn't make any sense."

"Maybe it was Tom's idea and not Grammy's."

"My thought, exactly! Can you come over later this morning and help me decide how to respond to this email?"

"Sorry, but I already have plans I can't cancel."

"It's important. I need to tell you about your daddy and me."

"That sounds serious, Mama."

"Well, there's more to our story now." Helen knows her parents are separated, but hasn't been told that their divorce papers have been signed and would be validated in six weeks—something new in Tennessee for uncontested divorces.

Evidently, a lot of marriages don't work.

"*More?* I'm coming over now, Mama."

"Forget I said anything, I'll figure things out for myself. Don't mess up your day for me, I'll be fine."

"No, I'm coming over now, Mama. Be there in thirty minutes. Don't go anywhere and turn the porch lights on."

Claire shudders, her divorce from Ted becoming more real.

"Should Ben be in on our conversation?" Helen asks. Her brother is a Certified Public Accountant for Cheatam County.

"No, no, Helen! I'll talk to him another time." Claire has another thought. "What will you tell Patrick?"

"Nothing. I'm here by myself. Free as a bird."

At Helen's statement, Claire's mind leaps to every wrong conclusion possible. He's left Helen. He's out with a hussy cheating on his beautiful wife. He's never coming back.

"Are you separated from Patrick?" Claire asks.

"Goodness no, Mama!" Helen exclaims. "He took the children camping overnight with several other fathers."

"Oh." Claire feels foolish for jumping to the worst conclusion. "I'm just not thinking clearly. Sorry."

My plight isn't hers.

"I know, Mama. That's why I'm coming over and spending the night. Put on some strong coffee and find us a good movie."

"Okay, honey, okay . . ." Claire ends the call, relieved.

* * *

Jess can't sleep. After all of John's sexual overtures he's too tired to act out his fantasies. She's in their king-size bed, facing the wall away from him. He's snoring gourds. That's unusual.

Something feels off with him. Maybe he's developed apnea. Can't that stop the heart for someone in their mid-sixties?

Jess listens to his uneven breathing. Slipping from the bed covers, she patters into the kitchen and stares out the bay window over the sink. The moon has risen and set, leaving darkness behind. It's already early Saturday. The mowers will roll over the golf green at sunrise so avid golfers can be playing by nine.

A noise prompts Jess to turn around.

"John, you startled me. Don't sneak up on me like that."

"I wasn't sneaking, Jessica. Why aren't you sleeping?"

"Why were you snoring? Do you have a cold?"

He leans a hand against a wall and bends over smiling.

"Something is different about you," Jess says.

He lifts his head and looks at her. Then, she knows.

"It's you, Joshua!" The dark inside of her thickens.

He rocks his head and laughs. "What gave me away?"

"That look," Jess says growing angry. "I've never seen that kind of look in my husband's gaze. You switched places."

"We did." Josh sits at the breakfast bar. "You won't tell John I let you get undressed in front of me, will you? I'll deny it."

"No. Why should he think any worse of his twin brother?"

"You were always the classy wench I let go in college," Josh says. "I should've married you instead of that witch, Rebecca."

"I was the one who left you, Josh."

Jess trembles, fearful for the first time since John left for Atlanta. The twin looks like her husband, but he has a mean streak. She would not put it past Josh to rape her then deny he did it. He steps closer and brushes Jessica's lips with his thumb.

"There's still time for you to cheat on your husband." He chuckles. "It would be fun, I promise you. I've practiced moves."

Jess slaps his hand away from her face. "Get out of my house, Josh. Now!" She dashes toward the door to the hall.

But Josh is faster and handily traps her.

"Come on, Jess. Did I sleep with you? I could have." He's grinning. "But I didn't. You are after all my brother's wife."

Jess struggles to loosen his hold on her.

"One kiss, and I'll sleep on the sofa."

Jess hauls back and slaps him hard on the cheek.

He rubs the redness away. "I guess that's a no, well, at least I tried. How many times has John tried lately? Trust him, do you?"

* * *

Claire raises the garage door to her house so Helen can come through the kitchen door. That's how Ted always entered. At the thought of him never coming home, a tear slips down one cheek.

The door opens. Helen has her own housekey.

"It's really dark out back, Mama. Do you have a security light out?" Helen walks over to the bar and plops down her purse.

"I forgot to ask your father to fix it."

"I presume he's not here." Helen tilts her head and listens for sounds. All she hears is the grunting AC cooling the house.

"Your daddy isn't coming back, ever!" Claire rounds the bar and pours two mugs of coffee. "Decaf. We need some sleep tonight after I tell you what's going on in this household."

Helen mounts a barstool. "You're scaring me, Mama."

When cream and a spoon of honey have been added to each coffee, Claire slides a mug down the bar to Helen.

"You already know that your daddy and I have suffered through marriage counseling," Claire says. "What I didn't tell you was that we stopped a month ago. Counseling wasn't working. He wants me to forgive him and fund his bastard son."

Helen startles. "That's pretty harsh, Mama. You can't blame a baby for Daddy's mistake." She does not want to take sides.

"Ted has chosen his bed, so now he'll have to lie in it."

"Is there more I should know?" Helen is weary from a busy work day. It's upsetting to hear how her parents have dismissed love so easily. The news is heart-breaking.

Claire takes a meditative sip of her decaf coffee and reveals, "I've signed the divorce papers. It will be final in six weeks."

"Just like that?" Helen shakes her head. "I know you love Daddy. Why can't you forgive him and let him come home?"

Claire stares at her daughter, so innocent about the sins of humankind. Not yet betrayed by someone she deeply loves.

"Even if Ted came home, he would never be all mine again, Helen. Half of him will always belong to Natalie and their son."

"I see . . ." Helen realizes there's nothing she can do to change anything. But June and Billy will suffer for their mistake.

"And there's another matter you need to know about."

Helen's blue eyes widen. "What can be worse than divorce?"

"Your grandmother may already be dead."

"What? Why do you think that?" Helen asks.

Claire sighs. "Thomas Kessler emailed me two weeks ago that he was sending Mama's ashes to Johnson Funeral Home."

"Okay . . ." Helen waits for more information.

"The ossuary was due to arrive at the funeral home a week ago on Friday. It didn't and I can't find out why."

Helen's angst rises. "Why haven't you said something before now? Do you think the package was stolen or just misplaced?"

Claire shakes her head. "I don't know, Helen. Both are a possibility." She intently locks eyes on her daughter.

"It seems odd Tom had Grammy cremated before talking to you," Helen offers. "There's something fishy about all of this."

"Absolutely, in lieu of the email I received today with explicit instructions how to carry out Mama's memorial service."

"Well . . ." Helen shakes her head, "that really stinks."

"What if Tom's lying?"

"Why would he say Grammy's dead when she isn't?"

"I don't know, Helen," Claire replies. "Lorene thinks I should have her daughter-in-law test the ashes for DNA."

"Are you referring to Dr. Cynthia Perkins?"

"Yes, like me, Lorene distrusts Thomas Kessler."

"But where are the ashes?" Helen exclaims.

18

GEORGE TAYLOR IS at the Columbia Post Office in the Mail Receiving Department early Monday, going through the recent parcel-post deliveries. One package of a particular size grabs his attention. He studies the postmark with the zip code 27925.

Columbus, North Carolina?

No, no, that is all wrong. This is the size of the package Post Master Beryl had instructed him to reroute to Langley, Virginia over a week ago. Who had sent it back from North Carolina?

And why? I'm going to get fired for mail tampering.

He should report this incident to—wait! Washington, D.C.? And interfere with federal business? If the Gov is involved, the U.S. Postal Service won't take kindly to his interference with internal business. So, what is he to do? He shakes his head.

Send it on and let the next person deal with it.

* * *

When Dr. Perkins returned from her coffee break late Monday morning, she spies a parcel addressed to Johnson's Funeral Home on her desk. Does it contain Dorothy Powell's ashes? The parcel is rectangular; about the size of an ossuary.

Hmm . . . Cyn meditates on her options. Maybe, the item is too controversial for Blake Johnson to deal with right now.

She slits the packaging tape to see if the ossuary with Dorothy's ashes is inside. Staring at the hot item, maybe she should talk to Blake first before doing anything with them.

No, her mother-in-law may know what's going on. She phones Lorene. "Mama? Your friend's ashes are here."

"Dorothy's?" Lorene exclaims.

"That's what the label says," Cyn clarifies.

Thinking she may have heard wrong, she utters, "I thought the urn was going straight to the Johnson's Funeral Home."

"Well, it's here now. Maybe the postal service sent it over."

"Who had the legal authority to change an address?"

"My thought, too. Maybe Blake Johnson sent it to the lab."

"Well, either way, I should tell Claire," Lorene decides. "She's been calling the funeral home twice a day about the ashes."

"Well, I won't touch these contents until a judge orders me to proceed with testing," Cyn declares. "Talk to Claire."

"Thanks for letting me know, Cyn. I'll phone Claire."

There is something fishy surrounding Dorothy's death.

* * *

Lorene ends the call with her daughter-in-law and phones Claire. "Your mother's urn has finally arrived in Columbia."

"At the funeral home?"

"No, Cyn called to let me know she has them at the lab."

"Tom said he was sending Mama's ashes to the funeral home," Claire reminds Lorene. "How did Cyn get the ashes?"

"She thinks Blake Johnson sent over the urn because of the mystery surrounding Dorothy's death. That's understandable."

"He doesn't want to bury my mother?" Claire is stressed over the situation. "Tell Cyn to go ahead and test the ashes for DNA."

"She won't do it without a court order, Claire."

"Well, I need to know for sure if my mother is dead, Lorene. Can you meet me at the Columbia Court House at two p.m.?"

"Why do you need me, Claire?"

"Support. We'll convince Judge Sewell to sign a court order giving the lab permission to test the ashes. I have to be sure."

"Doesn't fire destroy human tissue?"

"I need to start somewhere for my own sanity."

* * *

John Bailey did not get home from Atlanta until Monday afternoon. He found the house dirty and in disarray—not usually his wife's MO since she was spastic about abolishing germs.

Yesterday's dirty dishes were piled in the kitchen sink and tainted food odors lingered in the air. Magazines were scattered across the den. He pauses and listens for human sounds.

"Jess?" he calls out.

"Is that you, John?" She shakily enters the den, still wearing a housecoat over her nightgown. She's undone from Josh's ruse.

"I'm back, honey." He looks closely at her face streaked in red. "Is something wrong, Jess? Have you been crying?"

"Just not sleeping well since you left."

"Has something bad happened since I left for Atlanta?"

Jess stiffens. "You ask me that, John? After you switched places with Josh and sent him here without telling me'"'

He grins. "Oh, I see. This is about my naughty brother."

"Isn't everything about Josh these days?"

"He wanted to meet your Canasta friends and assess how much they knew about Dorothy's missing-in-action. Would you have agreed to cooperate if I had told you first?"

"Hell, no! He nearly ruined our cookout on Friday."

"I'm sorry. What did he do?"

It was what he did after they left that had upset Jess.

"I'm sorry, honey. Josh didn't tell me we were switching until I got to his apartment in Atlanta on Wednesday," he explains.

"You could have called and warned me, John."

"He said not to—that you would never allow him to spy on your buddies if you knew." He pauses. "Was it that bad?"

"He crawled in my bed Friday evening. I thought it was you."

John chuckles. "That cuss! We both fooled our teachers all the time, traded places and took tests for one another."

"He nearly raped me before I wised up, John."

"Oh, don't be so dramatic, sweetheart. Josh would never do that. He was just giving you a hard time." He shakes the coffee pot then looks at her. "Are leftovers from last night?"

"Forget about food or coffee. Josh saw me naked."

"Really?" Amused, his lips wiggle.

"Yes, really!" Her golden-brown eyes shoot arrows at him.

He grins and rocks his head. "Remind me, Jess, who did you sleep with first? Do you actually know for sure?"

Jess is livid. She wants to claw out John's eyes.

"This is not a game, John. This is our life. Your brother has messed up two marriages and the girl he's living with is half his age. I fear when I married you, I also married Josh."

"I see." John studies his wife. "Where is my brother?"

"He left sometime yesterday," she replies.

"Did he say where he was going?"

Jess actually grins. "I'm not your brother's keeper."

He laughs. "Well, wherever he is, it's nobody's business."

19

CLAIRE IS WAITING in the large foyer of the historic Columbia Courthouse when Lorene arrives. "Do we have an appointment?"

"No," Claire replies and they mount the stairs to the second floor. "I called ahead and told Judge Sewell's secretary what I needed." They walk down the long hallway together.

"Will he sign a Court Order to test Dorothy's ashes just like that?" Lorene snaps her fingers to punctuate the urgency.

"He better." Claire pushes open the door to the office.

Judge Sewell's secretary is busy at her computer. Claire clears her throat to gain attention. It doesn't work, so she grunts.

"Oh, hi, Claire." Sue Ann glances up, then drops her hands to her lap. "What can I do for you today?"

"I left you a message. Did you check your voicemail?"

"Yes, but the judge has been in court today." Sue Ann's eyes wander to her computer before noticing Lorene is in the room.

"Oh, hi, Ms. Perkins." She manages a weak smile.

"Hi, Sue Ann." Lorene glances over at Claire.

"Did you tell James I was coming?" Claire queries.

"No—judge keeps his cell phone turned off during court."

"Well, that stinks," Lorene mutters.

"I need a Court Order to have my Mama's ashes tested."

"No way I can help you with that!" Sue Ann barks. "Do you wanna leave Judge Sewell a message?"

"Tell me, Sue Ann, is James avoiding me?"

Her mouth tightens. "You'll have to ask him!"

"When?" Claire is persistent.

"My advice? Set an appointment." She resumes typing.

Dissatisfied, Claire complains loudly to Lorene until Sue Ann ceases work and abruptly pushes back from her desk.

"Mrs. Burkes, I'm not an attorney." The fake blond focuses droopy pale blue eyes. "But, you're welcome to wait."

"No thanks, we'll go now and be back by four."

"Your choice." Sue Ann resumes working.

"Let's go, Lorene," Claire says.

Outside the rear of the courthouse, the two women face each other on the sidewalk. It's too hot this afternoon. The atmosphere is loaded with plant pollen. Claire sneezes.

"Bless you!" Lorene calls out. "Too hot and humid for May. It's probably going to storm before bedtime."

"Before that, I intend to make my own thunder."

"It's 2:30, how are we going to kill some time?"

Claire thinks about killing the judge, then cautions herself. She is not her mother. She is not spastic nor a risktaker.

"Let's go over and talk to Blake Johnson," she suggests.

"Why?" Lorene asks.

"Tom emailed me early Saturday with a document attachment giving specific instructions how she wants to be memorialized."

"I swear, he keeps perpetuating the lie!" Lorene exclaims.

"He says Mama wants a party at the farm."

Lorene bursts out laughing.

"That's ludicrous! Dorothy doesn't own a farm anymore." She wipes sweat from her brow with a hand. "I need AC."

"Me, too. Before we go to the funeral home, I want an icy-cold drink." Coffee Call is catacorner across the street. "While we order, I'll phone Blake and tell him we're coming."

* * *

John teed off his golf game at 2 p.m. He was playing with three of his Poker buddies, Judge Sewell and the Attorney General of Tennessee, Joel Crafton. Bubba also took off work to play.

Jess is relieved to be alone in the house. It's time to clean up the mess from the past weekend and eliminate foul odors. Too hot to open windows, she sets the AC temp at 68.

While vacuuming the house, she recalls John's tenderness toward her after her meltdown over Joshua's behavior. She was young all over again as they romantically, insanely explored their feelings during a passionate love session on the den floor.

Then maybe hearing about Josh's naughty behavior on Friday had affected John. She can always tell when he's been with his twin. They seem to think and feel as one, and that is very scary.

And, to be honest, there are moments when she fantasizes about sleeping with Josh. She could have pretended he was John, and, well . . . the phone rings and interrupts Jess's insanity.

She grabs her cell. "Hello . . .?"

"It's me, Lorene. My friend Claire and I are about to order beverages at Coffee Call on the Square. We wondered if you wanted to drive over and meet us here for a visit."

"Sure." Jess looks at the time. "I can be there in fifteen."

"Want me to order you something?" Lorene asks.

"A double-smoothie with strawberries."

"See you soon . . ."

Jess hurriedly changes clothes and grabs the car keys from the hook by the door. She punches in the alarm code and enters the garage. John took the BMW, so she'll drive his Subaru Forester.

In the middle of the afternoon, traffic is light in Columbia, but will pick up around four when hospital shifts end and personnel head home. Jess locates parking across the street from the bistro, hops out of the SUV, and presses the fob to lock up.

Inside the bistro, the odors of coffees and pastries tease the palate. Jess had been to New Orleans numerous times with John and enjoyed a café au lait with beignets at Café Du Monde on Jackson Square. The owners of Coffee Call have done a great job with the décor, menu, and variations of gourmet coffee choices.

Jess sights Lorene, waves, and walks toward the table.

An attractive woman with fire-engine red hair sits across the table from Lorene. Dorothy Powell's daughter looks a lot like the picture she'd seen of her mother taken thirty years ago. Josh had provided John with a picture portfolio of Dorothy, some taken with family and friends. Some snapped at a spy's distance.

"Hi. Did I miss anything important?" Jess smiles.

"This is my new friend, Jessica Bailey." Lorene tells Claire. "She recently moved here and built a house on a golf course."

"Well, not me. My husband John hired an architect and contractor to do the job." Jess takes a seat at the table.

"Nice meeting you, Jessica." Claire smiles.

"My friends call me Jess," she says.

Their waitress arrives with their three drink orders.

"Which is mine?" Jess reads the labels on the tall cups.

"I had a cold cappuccino." Claire licks the foam off the top. "My mother always loved their hazelnut flavoring."

"I'm sorry to hear she's deceased." Jess selects the large-size cold cup with a slushy strawberry smoothie.

"We don't think Mama's dead," Claire says.

Lorene questions if she made a mistake by including Jess in their conversation about Dorothy's missing ashes. But it is the only way to discern if Jess is truly honest and sincere about fitting in with Columbia society. Tennessee folks think differently than city dwellers. Too many outsiders have passed through town and committed evil acts. Lorene feels it's her job to weed them out.

"Lorene and I decided to enjoy a treat while waiting to see Judge Sewell late afternoon. I need him to sign a Court Order to have my mama's ashes tested for DNA," Claire tells Jess.

"We don't trust the sender," Lorene whispers.

"By sender, you mean the person who mailed the ossuary." Jess nods, surprised she was included in such a personal matter.

But John will love hearing that news.

"Mama's significant-other sent it," Lorene pipes.

"She's dating?" Jess knew Dorothy was eighty-six.

"Dorothy had a facelift and doesn't look her age."

"Tom is Mama's friend," Claire interjects. "She trusts him."

"But you don't," Jess concludes.

"Not until the fire goes out in Hell!" Lorene remarks.

"Tom sent me an email saying he was sending Mama's ashes to the Johnson Funeral Home," Claire reveals to Jess.

"And you want to verify the ashes are your mother's."

"Yes," Claire replies. "I don't want to believe Mama is dead."

"Why would Tom lie?"

"Oh, an answer to that might take a century," Lorene pipes.

"I'd like to know more about you, Jess," Claire says.

"Sure. What do you want to know?"

"Lorene tells me you're filling in for my mother during their weekly Friday Canasta game at the Senior Citizen Center."

"That's right. Jane invited me. I love the game."

"Do you see your parents often?" Lorene inquires.

"No, they're deceased," Jess replies. "Mama had a stroke and Daddy died from heart disease. John's parents were killed in an automobile accident two years ago. Now that our daughter is deceased, it's just us. Well, and Joshua, John's twin brother."

"I'm sorry, Jess. Dealing with death is difficult," Claire empathizes. "Family is important. They are our life raft."

"I'm learning that friends are a huge benefit," Jess says.

"I agree. My girlfriends are my sisters," Lorene adds.

"What keeps John busy during retirement?" Claire asks.

"He golfs—plays Poker with friends Friday evenings," Jess answers. "If it will help, Claire, I'll ask John to talk to Judge Sewell about signing your court order to test Dorothy's ashes."

"Thank you, Jess. That's nice of you," Lorene interjects.

"I hope to have the paperwork before the day ends," Claire says. "If not, I'll be at James' door early tomorrow morning."

"James? You know him well," Jess concludes.

"Oh yes, he's been Mama's attorney for decades."

"So, tell me, Claire, do you have children?" Jess inquires.

"A son and daughter, and two grands."

"What keeps your husband busy?" Jess inquires.

"Claire is getting a divorce!" Lorene blares out.

"Oh." Jess reacts. "I'm so sorry."

Claire pushes out her lips. "Don't be. I'm the lucky one."

20

JUDGE SEWELL DID not return to his office Monday afternoon. Claire and Lorene refused to give up waiting until Sue Ann had her say. "He ain't coming back." She closes down her computer. "It's after five p.m., and I need to lock up and go home."

"Will he be here tomorrow morning?" Claire asks.

Sue Ann mouths, "Calendar says he will."

"But you don't really know, do you?" Lorene fusses.

"He's my boss, not the other way around."

"It's not your fault, Sue Ann," Clair declares to the judge's secretary. To Lorene, she mutters, "Let's get out of here."

Defeated, Lorene limps down the courthouse stairs thinking of how the Confederate army must have felt when Union Major General Joseph Hooker beat them badly in the Battle of Lookout Mountain during the Civil War. "But, it ain't over till it's over!"

"Lose today, win tomorrow!" Claire remarks. Exhausted from the long day, she dreads the hour drive back to Nashville.

Soon they are standing together on the sidewalk in back of the courthouse. "I'd better get on the road home before dark," Claire says as they begin walking toward Lorene's Tesla.

"Are you going to talk to your daughter-in-law tonight?" Claire asks. "She must wonder what Judge Sewell said about the court order." Dr. Cynthia Perkins is Maury County's coroner.

"Our trip to the courthouse was spontaneous," Lorene says. "I didn't tell her our plans. Besides, I have nothing to report."

It's hot outdoors, but a breeze stirs as the sun recedes.

"Stay the night with me." Lorene suggests.

"I don't want to impose."

"You're not. No use driving back to Nashville when you'll probably turn around and come back early in the morning."

"I probably shouldn't." Helen might worry.

"Say yes. We can be depressed together."

Claire chuckles. "I hope not, but that's a very tempting offer." She has no one waiting for her at home. "I understand now why Mama depended on you so much."

Lorene opens the passenger door, fills the seat, then looks up at Claire. "Forget about depression, we can strategize some more about the mysterious ashes. Judge Sewell can't put us off forever. And Jessica Bailey did say we could prevail on her husband John to help us. Get your car and follow me home."

"Okay, if it's not an imposition, I'll stay the night."

"That's what friends are for!" Lorene hails.

Claire is grateful. Tonight, she won't be alone.

"Better idea. Meet me at the house. I'll pick up food from Pizza Hut. We can relax, pig out, and watch an old Clark Gable movie. Dorothy and I often did that after our husbands died."

"Murdered on Crystal Creek!" Claire spurts. "That should be the name of my mother's book when she gets it published."

"She told you it's finished?" Lorene startles.

"No, but I read the notes she left in the guest nightstand. Pretty graphic details." Claire grins. "Mama didn't mince words."

There were romantic scenes between her and Tom.

"There isn't much your mother didn't do, Claire. She's had an exciting life, though dangerous. I hope she comes home soon."

"You sound so sure she's alive."

"It's important we stay positive."

"I agree."

"See you back at the house."

* * *

Jess is home by four p.m. She had stopped by Kroger and bought a few grocery items. As she let herself into the kitchen through the garage entrance, she hears men's voices.

"Jessica! Have you met Joel Crafton?"

"No." Jess shakes the Attorney General's hand. "But I've heard some good things about you from John."

"Hello, Jess," Judge Sewell calls out from the kitchen.

Seated on a barstool, he holds a clear glass of liquid. Vodka: the kind that leaves no breath odor and still has a buzz.

"Good to see you again, Judge. How is Grace? I heard she was having some health issues." Jess sets her purse on the kitchen cabinet next to the fridge. "Arthritis, the girls at the County Club Garden Club tell me. I should call her and we'll do lunch."

"I wish you would, Jess. It might lift her spirits."

"Oh . . ." Jess adds, "I ran into Claire Burkes today. She said she had an appointment with you late this afternoon."

"What about?" John asks.

"Something about a Court Order to test her mother's ashes."

"Why?" Joel interjects. "Is there a suspicion it's not her?"

"Dorothy Powell," the judge identifies the name of the person they are discussing. "Her urn is expected anytime. It's my understanding she's already been identified and cremated."

Jess is on a rabbit chase. "Her daughter doesn't trust the source who emailed her about her mother's death."

"Claire Burkes is the daughter," the judge says, almost angrily.

"Yes, but I would want to know, too." Jess looks at Sewell. "To me, it's the decent thing to do for the family."

John adds, "I think so, too, James. Be kind and let Claire have the ashes checked just to be sure they are her mother's."

The judge frowns. Now, he doesn't have a choice.

John winks at Jess. They work well together.

"Oh, Judge Sewell, it's my understanding the urn arrived earlier today—at the coroner's office," Jess adds.

"Why wasn't I informed?"

Jess says, "Ask your secretary."

21

TUESDAY MORNING, LORENE is nuking bacon in the microwave for breakfast when her cell phone dances on the counter. She still has it on vibration for the night.

"Hello!" She grabs the phone and answers.

"Good morning, Mama. I've been trying to reach Claire Burkes this morning and she's not answering her phone."

Lorene looks at Claire, seated at the breakfast bar across from her, mouthing a question: *Who is it?*

"Why are you looking for Claire?" Lorene waves off Claire's questions. "Is this about Dorothy's ashes?"

"That's part of the reason why I need to talk to her, Mama. Is there another way for me to contact her?"

Background noises muffle Cyn's words.

"Would you repeat that?"

"I need to get in touch with Claire Burkes!"

"You don't have to scream, Cyn, I'm not deaf."

"Sorry, Mama. I have news about the ashes."

"Don't tell me, Cyn. Claire is sitting right here in front of me." Lorene hands over her phone. "It's my daughter-in-law."

"Yes?" Claire tentatively answers.

"Can you come to the lab now?"

"Sure, why?" Claire locks eyes on Lorene.

"I'll explain when you get here."

The call falls dead.

"What did she want?" Lorene asks as she removes the crisp bacon from the microwave and pours off the excess drippings.

"She wants me to come to the lab."

"Did she say why?"

"Only that she would explain when I get there."

Humph. Lorene parks a hand on one hip. "Maybe it means Cyn discovered a new technique to identify the ashes."

"What if the remains are my mother's?" Claire worries.

"Okay, I'll drive you to the lab and we can both hear what Cyn has to say," Lorene pipes. "But first, we'll have breakfast."

* * *

Agent Joshua Bailey left his brother's house last Saturday and took a direct flight out of Nashville to the CIA headquarters in the George Bush Center for Intelligence. Director Jackson Carlton was expecting him. Jack closes his office door as soon as Josh is seated in front of his desk. The two men glare at one another.

"What have you learned about Dorothy Powell?"

Josh grins. The Director is always direct.

"Her closest friends don't accept her death."

"You base that opinion on what?" Jack adjusts the blinds to cut out the glaring sunlight. "Give me an example."

Josh removes his phone from his pocket. He'd taped the conversations that occurred on Friday evening at the cookout.

Jack listens to the parley between Dorothy's three friends and Josh. "Lorene Perkins, the ring leader? How do you read her?"

"She never admitted not accepting Dorothy's death, but her facial expressions revealed a number of emotions. She's upset that Dorothy might be dead, but I don't believe she trusts it's true."

"I see." The Director faces the window overlooking a park below. He'd rather be having a brunch in D.C. than dealing with the Dorothy issue. "Well, we did something about that."

Josh walks over to the window and stands next to Jack.

"Are you referring to the missing urn?"

"Yes, I had the Columbia Post Master redirect the ashes to a post office box in Langley. Our technician removed some of ashes and tested for DNA. There wasn't any. So, we added some."

Josh waits for more information; arms crossed as he gazes down at the park below. He can't stop thinking about Jessica since the night he saw her naked. She is so . . . beautiful.

"I want Dorothy scattered in Columbia," Jack says.

"But do we really know if she's dead?" Josh asks.

"No way to confirm it, unless we locate Thomas Kessler. No doubt Dorothy's death was his plan—to stop us from harming her again." Jack walks back to his desk and retrieves a folder.

"What is this?" Josh flips it open.

"Your next assignment. We believe Tom and Dorothy are hiding out in Central America. Our tech guy has done some research and backtracked where the package originated."

"That's pretty cool," Josh says, grinning.

"Belize, on the Gulf of Honduras. Go there and find Tom. If Dorothy Powell is breathing, she is hiding out with him."

"Yes, sir."

"My secretary has your flight information. Good hunting."

* * *

Early Tuesday, Claire and Lorene were seated in front of Dr. Cynthia Perkins' desk cluttered with folders. Cyn appeared perplexed. "What's wrong, Dr. Perkins? Is my mama dead?"

"Let me start at the beginning and we'll talk about it."

Lorene looks at Claire. "That means there's doubt."

Cyn sits on the lip of her desk in front of the two women. "I received the Court Order around 8 a.m. this morning, giving me permission to perform a DNA test on the urn's ashes."

"Okay, that's progress." Claire sits up straight. "Sue Ann came through for us." She high-five's Lorene.

"Don't keep us in suspense!" Lorene barks. "Tell us!"

"I did find something that indicates a match to Dorothy's DNA," Cyn reports. "She was once arrested for a crime."

"So, the Double-D-D police have my Mama's DNA?" Claire explodes. "She was proven innocent of killing my daddy."

Cyn raises a hand. "Calm down, Claire. It's a good thing I had a sample to compare the ash to, or," she stops short.

"Or what?"

"I would not have been able to confirm if the ashes were Dorothy's." She notes tears streaming down Claire's cheeks.

"So, my friend is dead." Lorene is horrified.

"Don't' rush me, Mama. I also weighed the ashes."

"You did?" Claire perks up, hope rising.

"Why?" Lorene inquires.

"Why does my mother's weight matter?" Claire asks.

Cyn holds up a hand to silence the women.

"I'm getting to my point, girls. Pay attention."

"We are!" they answer simultaneously.

"How much did Dorothy weigh before she left?" Cyn asks.

Claire's blue eyes flash with recall. "Well, she had a complete physical last year in October. But she put on some weight after getting out of the mental hospital," she recalls. "And she's been away from Columbia for the past six months."

"Just guestimate, Claire," Cyn says.

"One forty? She's five ten, slender."

"Okay . . ." Cyn rounds her desk and closes the folder containing the report. Something is definitely amiss.

"Okay, what?" Claire stands, a frown materializing.

"If this is your mother's remains, then someone has removed part of the ashes," Cyn declares. "Or, it isn't Dorothy."

"What makes you think that? Lorene points a bony finger.

"This person would have to weigh 120 pounds before cremation. I don't think Dorothy lost that much weight in six months unless she's been ill." Cyn pauses.

"What?" Claire utters.

"To verify that, we'd have to talk to Thomas Kessler."

"I tried emailing him back," Claire says. "He's closed that email account. Something really fishy is going on."

"It's about the book she's writing. The CIA will do anything to keep the public from knowing about the money they withdrew from international bank accounts. Money Tom's deceased wife had deposited decades ago," Lorene says. "He forced Dorothy to close those accounts then gave the money back to the feds."

Cyn gazes at Lorene. "Has this ever been made public?"

"No," Claire answers. "I read about some of it in my mother's notes she keeps locked in a bedside table drawer."

"I see, so you sneaked a look?" Cyn assumes.

"After she ran off. But the notes aren't there anymore."

"How is that possible?"

"Someone must have taken them when I was away from the house." Claire bursts out in tears. "This is all messed up."

"Don't cry, honey." Lorene hugs her. "The girls and I will figure it all out. Your mother was a really good teacher."

"Thank you, Lorene." Claire dries her eyes on her shirttail.

"Besides, I still have Dorothy's letter she sent me."

"What letter?" Both Claire and Cyn cooperatively ask.

"I heard from her two weeks ago," Lorene says.

"About the time the urn was due to arrive at the post office," Cyn recalls. "But the parcel wasn't delivered until a week later."

"George Taylor told his wife he sent it to Langley, Virginia," Lorene reveals. "It doesn't take a rocket scientist to figure out that the blame feds messed with the ashes then sent them here."

"Your Canasta Club figured all that out?" Cyn is impressed.

"Of course, we did! We're old but not stupid."

Claire suppresses a smile. Lorene sounds like her mother.

"I bet my bottom dollar they found no proof that Dorothy is dead," Lorene speculates. "They planted DNA to make us believe she's dead." What awful trauma Dorothy must be going through.

"I think you're right, Lorene. Mama is hiding out somewhere with Thomas Kessler. She believes he's the only one who can protect her," Claire says. "How are we going to get her back?"

"I don't know," Lorene replies. "We'll figure it out."

"You girls in the club," Cyn says, nodding her head.

"I believe you, Lorene," Claire says. "Thank you."

"My pleasure."

22

FRIDAY ROLLS AROUND and it's time for the Canasta game at the Senior Citizen Center to begin. Jessica Bailey is first to arrive and take her seat at the table for four on the back patio. She is still upset with John. Although he'd tried to appease her with sex, it did not negate the fact he'd so easily dismissed the fact that Josh had seen her naked, and worse, crawled into bed with her. He has no idea what Josh did to her long ago. A secret that haunts her.

"What's wrong, dear?" Lizzy asks as she joins Jess at the Canasta table. "Did you burn John's supper last night?"

"Worse than that, Liz, but I prefer to let that baby rest."

"I understand. The girls and I are dealing with our own trauma. So much has happened this week to trouble us."

"What has happened?" Jess sits back in her chair, arms crossed. "Is this about your missing friend, Dorothy?"

"I don't know if I should say anymore."

"Any more about what?" Jane stands between them.

"About Dorothy, and the, you know. . ."

"I don't think if matters if we tell Jess what's going on," Jane speculates as she sits across from Jess. "Where is Lorene?"

"She'll be here." Jane shuffles the cards. "As soon as she returns from Ellie Peters' farm." She looks at Lizzy.

"Who is Ellie?" Jess inquires.

"Ellie was once married to the detective that Dorothy despised because he almost raped her daughter Claire when she was in the ninth grade," Jane answers Jess's question.

"After Butch Peters was murdered, actually set on fire by an assassin, Ellie purchased Dorothy's farm," Lizzy interjects.

"Goodness, girls! It's more dangerous to live here than Alanta." Horror mars Jess's pretty face. "How many have died?"

"I don't think anybody knows the total body count." Jane places the fifty-two cards in the caddy. "A lot of innocents."

Lizzy glances at her wristwatch. "Lorene's late."

"She'll be here!" Jane says. "Or phone if she can't be."

Jess grins. "I love the way you girls cover for each other. I had a friend like that back in Atlanta. We were joined at the hip since college days, but she contracted Lupus and died." Sadness courses her expression. "I guess we all suffer losses."

"Who's lost?" Lorene hustles toward the table.

"Not you, thank God!" Lizzy hails.

"Did I miss anything?" Lorene looks down at the girls. "Sorry I'm running late. Hi, Jess. What did I miss?"

"We were just telling Jess about Ellie Peters," Jane says as Lorene sits across from Lizzy. "How was your visit?"

"Exactly what did you tell Jess about Ellie?"

"That she bought Dorothy's farm," Lizzy replies.

"And her detective husband is deceased," Jane adds.

"Butch Peters was a piece of work!" Lorene barks.

"I think we scared Jess about the murders that occurred in Columbia after my Crawford and Arthur Powell died," Lorene reveals. "I'm sorry, Jess. We're a pretty calm town now."

Lorene gazes at Jess. "I went over to Ellie's with Claire Burkes to plan her mother's memorial service."

"So, you believe Dorothy is deceased." Jess nods.

Lorene's gaze flitters between Jane and Lizzy.

"You'd rather not say, I get it," Jess says.

Complete silence floods the atmosphere.

"Shouldn't we tell Jess about our plan?" Jane asks.

Jess raises a hand. "Honestly, girls, I don't want to intrude."

"You're not, Jess. You live here now. You are one of us. All we want to do is find Dorothy and make sure she's safe." Jane knows Jess will be replaced at the table by Dorothy if she returns.

"I understand your hesitancy," Jess says. "I'm new to Columbia and you are still evaluating my sincerity."

"We don't want you to feel like an outsider."

"Thank you, Jane. Really, I know I'm substituting for Dorothy until she comes home. I understand your concern."

"Thank you for that," Lorene pipes.

"You're so sweet, Jess. You've been our blessing."

"Thank you, Jane." Jess suffers guilt. She'd been snooping on them for John. But isn't it time to forge honest relationships?

"Okay, I'm dealing the cards." Jane begins.

The conversation about Dorothy ceases as the game proceeds and the two teams play hard to win. They are finished by 4:15 p.m. Jane puts the cards away. They head for the door.

"Why don't we all go out for supper somewhere tonight?"

"That's a great idea, Lorene!" Lizzy hawks.

"You're invited, too, Jess," Jane adds.

"Are you sure?"

"Yes," Lorene decides. "Jane trusts you, so why shouldn't I? Besides, I've been keeping something from all of you."

"What?" Jane startles.

"A need-to-know basis," Lorene replies.

"Okay, time to share the details," Lizzy insists.

"I need to tell you about the letter Dorothy sent me two weeks ago," Lorene says as they enter the parking lot.

"What did she say?" Jane asks.

"Okay, but before I tell you, where do we want to eat?"

"Somewhere quiet and private," Lizzy suggests.

"We don't need rumors getting started," Jane adds.

"There's a new restaurant at the discount mall that just opened," Jess reveals. "I've heard the food is great."

"Okay," Lorene agrees. "We can order something healthy there, and I'll tell you what I found out from Dorothy."

"We should carpool," Jess suggests. "You can ride with me."

"Is there room?" Jane inquires.

"I'm driving John's SUV, so yes."

The new discount mall is located five miles south of the Columbia off I-65. It has raving food reviews on the Net. The owner and chef are from New York City. Facebook reports that Joseph knows how to whip up pizza dough that's uncontested.

23

JESS IS A GOOD driver. The girls exit the SUV and enter Sam's Pizza Parlor. "I thought you said we were eating healthy food," Jane whispers to Lorene as they locate a table for four.

"It is healthy. Choose a veggie pizza," Lizzy tells Jane.

"We can share a big salad," Lorene suggests.

"Well, at least I don't see anybody I know," Jess says.

"Well, that's not saying a lot since you're new to the area," Lorene comments. "Sorry, that didn't come out right."

"I know . . ." Jess says. "I am new to Columbia."

The girls study the laminated menu. A variety of red and white sauces are listed if you build your own prize pizza. It's early for supper, but elderly couples come through the door in droves.

"So much for quiet and private," Lorene mutters.

After ordering two large deluxe pizzas to share, the girls have enough left over to take home with them. Lorene suggests meeting at her house so they can air their dirty underwear.

By that, she meant their grievances regarding Dorothy's ashes and her attachment to CIA Agent Thomas Kessler. The Big Zero.

Lorene pays the tab for the pizzas and large salad. It takes another forty-five minutes to get to her house five miles north of Columbia. Jane and Lizzy want ice cream for dessert.

Jess declines, but she'll have decaf coffee. By then it is well after 9 p.m. Jane and Lizzy are yawning. Jess looks weary, too.

"Okay, Jess, I need to fill you in on Dorothy's background," Lorene begins. "Her drama started six years ago."

"That's a lot of filling in," Jane says, yawning.

"Arthur and Dorothy Powell owned the farm next to mine before Ellie Simpson bought it—a long story which I will skip for now." Lorene looks at Jess. "Anyhow, my Crawford and Arthur played poker with other business men in Colombia on Fridays. Arthur's farm assistant usually came with him to play cards."

Lizzy nods off over the buzz of conversations.

"Okay, Jane, take Lizzy home if she's not going to listen."

Lizzy's eyes snap open. "I need caffeine."

"Jane, make us some real coffee," Lorene orders.

Jess rolls her hand for Lorene to continue.

"Clyde Willems was Arthur's help with the farm—he's dead, too. Also murdered." Lorene sucks in a breath. "Clyde told Crawford a dangerous secret that upset some bad people, so they both took out life-insurance policies naming their wives as the recipients. Me and Dorothy, just in case things went south."

"They were afraid for their lives?" Jess wants clarification.

"Darn toot'in they were. The Russian Mafia sent in an assassin to kill them." Lorene pauses. "At first, the police believed Dorothy murdered her husband on Crystal Creek for the policy."

"That's awful!" Jess utters.

"Then my Crawford died—also on Crystal Creek." Tears materialize. "I suspected he was murdered, too, but no proof turned up," Lorene reveals. "It was a devastating year, but Dorothy and I became close friends. She helped me so much."

Jess listens, not knowing what questions to ask.

"Thomas Kessler saw Dorothy's picture in *The Tennessean*. He worked for the CIA, and arranged to be hired as the manager of our Senior Citizen Center, posing as Clint Howard."

The coffee bubbles out in the decanter.

"Everyone, get a cup," Lorene says. "Cream is in the fridge."

"Anyhow, Clint was really here to woo Dorothy."

"Like, seduce her into a sexual relationship?" Jess says.

"Oh, pshaw!" Lizzy coughs out. "Dorothy is a good Methodist. She would never sleep with Tom."

"But she wanted to," Lorene interjects. "Tom involved her in all kinds of illegal nonsense, even once kidnapped her."

"Why did Tom target Dorothy?" Jess asks the obvious.

"She resembled his first wife, Angela, a double-agent for the CIA and Russian SRV," Lorene explains. "Dorothy was a fool for love. What happened to her was enough to write a book!"

"So . . .?" It's late and she needs to beat John home.

"So, the letter Dorothy sent me two weeks ago," Lorene continues. "Mind you, she left Columbia over six months ago without telling anyone where she was going. Now, we know for sure she's been with Thomas Kessler," Lorene continues.

"What exactly did the letter say?" Jane inquires.

"That the CIA is paranoid about the book she is writing. They don't want their shenanigans regarding the large sums of money she withdrew from international banks to be exposed to the public." Lorene pauses to reflect on how much to disclose.

"We won't tell a soul what you tell us," Lizzy utters.

"Yeah, just like Postal George kept his secret about the ashes Tom sent to Columbia!" Lorene exclaims, waving a hand. "I know, I can trust you. Just saying promises are hard to keep."

"Did Dorothy ask you to keep a promise?" Jess asks.

"I take the fifth!" Lorene exclaims.

Jess is blown away. No wonder Josh has John looking into Dorothy's whereabouts. The CIA would never let that book see the light of day if it tarnishes their good reputation around the world. How can she admit to the girls she's been spying, too?

"Well, if I know Dorothy, she's found a way to outsmart the feds. We just have to keep our eyes and ears open for news."

"Thank you, Jane. You always were the sane one in our club," Lorene says. "Keep praying Dorothy will be safe."

"Done!" Lizzy widely yawns.

24

LORENE DECIDED TO end her story of Dorothy with only the tip of the knife, so to speak. She knew much more about where her friend was hanging out and the danger the CIA proposed.

That is why Dorothy trusted her to sneak into Claire's house in Nashville and steal the book notes from the guest bedroom's locked drawer. Dorothy mailed the key, so she hadn't actually broken in. Plus, the notes belonged to Dorothy, not Claire.

Jane and Jess had already left, but Lizzy sits at the bar half-asleep, but not making a move to leave Lorene's house.

"Why aren't you going home, Lizzy?" Lorene asks.

"You didn't finish the story, about the letter."

"I said all I wanted to." Lorene loaded their dirty dessert dishes in the dishwasher. "What do you want to know?"

"Was she still with Tom when she mailed the letter?"

"She didn't say specifically," Lorene replies, leaning forearms on the bar as she sleepily glares at Lizzy.

"Why didn't you tell Jess and Jane that?"

Lorene stiffens. "Is this an interrogation, Lizzy?"

"No, it's called sharing information with a good friend."

"Okay, okay," Lorene waves her off. "I presume Dorothy is with Tom. She doesn't have the skill set to stay alive without his help," Lorene states. "We just need to trust her instincts."

"Why hide out in Belize?" Lizzy wonders.

"I have no idea. Maybe she's enjoying a vacation."

"You know more, Lorene. Please tell me," Lizzy pleads.

"Okay, she did say in her letter that Tom had phoned her a few days before she left Columbia and told her she was in danger. She's sorry she didn't tell us she was leaving. The rest is history."

"Why didn't she trust us?" Lizzy's feelings are wounded.

"She trusts me more, Lizzy. And now, the Double D-D CIA has sent a spy to Columbia to find out what we know."

"Okay." Lizzy gets it. "If the CIA thinks Dorothy is dead, they'll stop looking for her. We just need to play along."

"Exactly! That's why I went with Claire over to Ellie Simpson's house today—to plan Dorothy's memorial service!" Lorene announces. "We have to convince the feds that she's dead so they'll quit sending spooks to our town to spy on us."

* * *

Jess had let Jane off at the Senior Citizen Center where she'd left her car. Home by 10:15 p.m., she'd beat her husband home.

No telling how late John would play poker at Judge Sewell's house. As long as the guys were drinking and talking, he would stay to hear if the subject of Dorothy Powell came up again.

Tired from the day, Jess sheds her clothes for a nightgown and reads a novel in bed till nearly midnight. When her eyelids droop, she closes her book, rolls over, and turns out the lights.

Should I tell John about the letter Lorene received? Surely, Josh knew more than she did, and had told John.

No. She likes her new friends. John would not have moved to Nashville if their daughter wasn't dying from cancer.

Now they owned a home in Columbia.

When she found out John only settled here to spy on behalf of his brother, she found it hard to believe. John had always been a fool for his twin and do anything he asks.

But she has no expectation Josh will reciprocate. He is a selfish SOB and would never change

How can identical twins be so different?

25

PLANS WERE SET FOR Dorothy's memorial service on Saturday, May 29. Claire, with Lorene's help, had decided to produce a memorial service for her mother the town would never forget. Tom had emailed the instructions—no doubt orchestrated by Dorothy. It was an attempt to convince the CIA she was dead.

Deader 'n a doornail! Lorene had declared.

Dr. Cynthia Perkins had tested the ashes and confirmed they could not possibly be Dorothy's remains due to their weight.

Still, the unknowns are troubling.

At least Claire now knew that Lorene had removed the book notes from her house. She recalls their conversation.

"You broke into my house?"

"No, your mama sent me a key to your house. Besides, I knocked first," Lorene explains. "Helen let me in."

"Did you tell Helen why you were there?"

"No, I lied, Claire. Dorothy would have done the same."

Lorene was right, and she never wavered in her belief that her best friend was alive. Thomas Kessler was with her, and would protect her with his life. Somehow, her mother would outsmart the CIA and bring justice to America. Still, Claire had no peace.

It is after midnight Saturday morning and she has not slept a wink. Her thoughts are heavy over the situation. And she is still very sad that Ted had left her for a younger woman.

* * *

Meanwhile, CIA plans were unfolding in the City of Belize as Agent James Grossman exits the international airport, posing as a tourist. He wears shorts and a Hawaiian print shirt bright as the jungle sunrise casting long shadows over the bustling city.

He walks briskly out into the open theater of visitors and hails a cab to a rundown hotel on the outskirts of Belize. With him is a zippered gaberdine tennis-shaped bag holding a sniper rifle. He's had plenty of target practice over the past two decades since he was first an army sniper before working for the CIA.

Once, he'd been sent to Paris, France, to approach Dorothy Powell in a public park. He'd offered her a chance to escape from Thomas Kessler and his scheme to force her to remove millions of American dollars from international banks. She'd refused.

Which meant she was complicit with Tom.

Jim had Dorothy's face memorized. Tom could not protect her forever. The CIA had eyes in every corner of the world, their tax dollars spent well on the right thugs. He grins, also aware that Agent Joshua Bailey had been sent to find Dorothy and bring her back alive to Langley headquarters. Jim would not let that happen.

But Josh didn't know that.

Dorothy is dangerous to the CIA, bent on exposing their corruptive behavior around the world. If Josh captured her first, Director Carlton would negotiate a lucrative payoff in exchange for the book and notes—more loot than she could possibly earn in two lifetimes. But the Director, like Jim, knew that she would not take the deal. So, an alternate plan had been set into motion.

Find Dorothy. Kill her. Ask questions later.

Jim loves his corrupt job. Since Dorothy's family and friends already believe she is dead, a quick bullet will serve justice.

* * *

Summertime is approaching in Central America. May's temps' range between mid-90s at noon to low 70s at night. Rainfall in the jungle averages 4.88 inches per month. The terrain is beautiful.

Dorothy Powell shares a rustic tree-house with Tom. Rent is reasonable since the structure is not air-conditioned. However, the breeze blowing through the tangle of trees off the Caribbean Sea cools the house constructed of wood with a thatched roof.

And the house is roomy enough for Dorothy to have a separate bedroom. She shares a living area, a bathroom, and a kitchen with Tom. On the covered back porch, he has satellite equipment set up for communication. Tom likes to keep abreast of world affairs. And he has a snoop at the Langley CIA office.

Even Dorothy doesn't know *her* name.

The kitchen cooktop and fridge are adequate. Overhead cabinets are stocked with canned items and dry spices. Plus, Tom shops twice a week for fresh vegetables and meats in a small village closest to San Ignacio, one of the five largest cities in the Country of Belize. When he shops, he's always disguised.

He looks adorable in ragged jeans, a plaid cotton shirt, and an old yellow straw hat. The worn-out wagon he drives is pulled by two old mules he'd purchased from a local farmer. Dadgum if the experienced CIA agent didn't fit anywhere like fleece on a lamb.

Only Tom is a wolf in sheep's clothing.

Romeo can charm a snake into his bed and the serpent wouldn't bite, he is so adorable. That Dorothy loves him to fault is a huge problem. He keeps on begging her to marry him.

"No," she'd told him.

But that was over six months ago, before he'd sent her a ticket to the City of Belize and said not to tell even Claire. He'd warned that the CIA would come after her now that she'd become public about writing her thriller. After she'd done an interview on Channel 5 in Nashville, Tennessee, and told the public her intent to reveal the CIA's secrets, they had angrily reacted.

"Honey, the CIA wants you dead."

"Good luck with that!" She'd laughed it off.

So, she has been hiding out in the Central America jungle with Tom until it is safe to return to the USA. He says that might be never. Marry him. He'll protect her. He's already purchased a remote island where they can live out their lives in peace.

"Please? Pretty please?"

After a month of plotting, they had devised a workable plan to convince the CIA that she was deceased. If successful, the feds would stop looking for her and let them enjoy their retirement.

"Forget about the book, honey. Live in the moment."

She hates when Tom calls her 'honey.' It makes her melt like chocolate in sunlight. Every fiber in her body wants to hug him and never let go. She is actually working on her wedding vows.

I vow to be the boss and never let you win.

This is a joke, so Tom laughs every time he recalls her statement. She means it, but with Tom, who knows?

* * *

Agent Jim Grossman doesn't like his living quarters at the rundown City of Belize motel built during the 1950s. But Director Carlton had told him to keep a low profile while looking for Dorothy Powell. He has no intention of confronting her or Tom.

When he was told to find Dorothy and take care of the problem, that meant his job was to shut her up forever.

One kill shot and Dorothy will be silenced.

One other thing: Thomas Kessler had to die, too.

That was on Jim because of their jaded past.

Back during the Gulf War, they had served together in a special sniper unit. Jim felt betrayed when Tom reported to their colonel that he'd shot two children at a village they had scoped out. The kid had a gun, Jim had reasoned. He was only protecting them. But Tom hadn't seen it that way. He'd called him "a loose cannon who did not deserve to serve in the U.S. Army."

Jim never forgave him. Not long after his unit returned to the states, he was romanced by the CIA as a sniper. The pay was so significant he couldn't turn down the job. In France, the time he'd tracked down Dorothy in the public park, he'd considered killing her then, but his mission was to coax her to Langley.

Even that, he'd failed at—but not this time.

A listening device installed in Claire Burkes cell phone taped Dorothy's last conversation with her mother over seven months ago. Dorothy had not told her mother she was leaving Tennessee.

The old woman was intelligent, clever, and tricky.

Jim also knew that Dorothy's ticket out of Nashville was not for the City of Belize. When she got to the Nashville airport, a messenger sent by Tom confronted her with an envelope. It was a ticket to Mexico City. Since her name was not registered on any VISA of incoming passengers, it is obvious she used a fake name.

Tom had met her at the airport in Mexico City and they had flown in a small plane into the heart of the Belize jungle. The CIA had a snoop at every major airport in the world. It is impossible to hide from the Agency forever. But Tom somehow had managed.

Sending Dorothy's cremated ashes in an urn from the City of Belize was intended to throw the feds off their trail. The CIA would assume they had left the country after that. But Jim's tracker instinct told him he was on the right trail to their demise.

They are here and I will find them.

26

Saturday, May 29

ELLIE SIMPSON IS HOSTING the Memorial Service at the farm she purchased from Dorothy Powell. A week ago, online invitations had gone out to friends, including First Methodist Church members. Brother Kenny will conduct the service.

The event was coordinated with Claire Burkes, Dorothy's daughter, and Lorene Perkins. Many who knew the Powells had offered to help. Bubba the Barber had sent over a lawn crew to mow the front and back yards and trim the tree branches, claiming he'd known the Powells well. Decorative pots with greenery artfully displayed in the front yard came from Joan's Nursery, and Jessica Bailey, a newcomer, had hired a violinist and cello player.

Dorothy's Canasta buddies provided the tablecloth and paper products. Bark's Seared Pork is catering the meal—including pork barbeque, buns, slaw, and potato salad. Coffee Call sent over a large carafe of their best coffee brew with a variety of desserts since Dorothy was a regular patron. Early this morning, Claire helped Ellie clip family pictures to a clothesline strung between the house and a tree. Lorene checks her list for progress.

The food will be served on the long table under the shade of the large oak tree. At one end sits a large container of lemonade with a self-serve spicket for guests to enjoy as they mingle before the meal is served. Claire wants her guests to fraternize before they enjoy a meal, hear a eulogy from Pastor Kenny, then witness the scattering of her mother's ashes over the grassy field where Arthur Powell had spent so much of his time tending his cattle.

At 11:30, guests begin arriving. Lorene's son, Ben, with some of his fire-fighting buddies begin parking the vehicles behind the barn. Ellie's front and back doors are open to guests who need the bathroom, or have never been inside the place where Arthur and Dorothy had lived most of their married lives. It's time to begin.

Claire welcomes everyone from the stage lectern using a microphone set up by the local radio station. Brother Kenny pronounces a beautiful prayer over both the food and Dorothy's family. Claire even sheds a few tears, unsure if her mother is alive.

Afterall, this whole shindig is a trick to fool the CIA.

* * *

Back in Belize

"You're back!" Dorothy exclaims as Tom climbs the ladder to the tree-house. "What did you purchase at the market?"

He holds a .44 pistol and a pack of cartridges in his hands.

She squints her eyes and mutters, "We can't eat that."

"Forget about food. Get packed, we're moving."

"What?" She splays her hands. "Why? I'm happy here."

"But you're not safe, Dorothy."

"Since when? What changed?"

"The CIA has found us," Tom reveals as Dorothy trails him into his messy bedroom. "Okay, so where are we going?"

He spins around. "Away, dear. Not sure yet."

Dorothy drops her butt on the bed. "You're moving too fast for me, Tom. What's going on?" Fear cascades through her.

Won't they ever give up?

Tom tosses a few clothes in a suitcase and looks up.

"Why aren't you in your bedroom packing? An assassin is on his way here to kill us. What is it you don't get, Dorothy?"

Tom can strike fear in a tiger.

"Okay, I'll pack. But you have some explaining to do."

"Okay, honey. You know I love you."

He better—for what he puts me through.

* * *

Jim Grossman is driving a jeep. He'd just learned from the manager that one of his tree-houses was rented to Clint Howard. His customer had recently paid cash to extend his six-month lease for two more months. The American woman with him, a redhead, was a real looker for her age. Brenda something, he recalled.

Jim had chuckled and given the manager a healthy tip for the info, then said, "I need the GPS coordinates to the tree-house. I heard they were getting married, so I have a present for them."

Then Jim paid him another fifty not to tell anybody.

It had taken Jim an hour to reach the two-bedroom tree-house tucked away in a thicket of jungle. It is hot as Hades today. Sweat pours off his skin even in a sleeveless cotton shirt and a pair of khaki shorts. Stealthily approaching the wooden structure from the back, Jim climbs the ladder and flattens himself against the porch wall. He listens for sounds. Nothing for a few seconds.

Then he hears a woman's voice. "I'm ready to go, Tom."

Sweet! This should be like picking grapes from a vine.

* * *

Back at Ellie's farm in Maury County Tennessee, thirty-nine of Claire's guests have fixed their lunch plates and found seats in the folding chairs scattered under the branches of the large oak.

The weather is perfect this afternoon. Not too hot with a gentle breeze blowing across the lawn. Claire thanks God for the beautiful day, praying her wandering mother is safe, and that CIA Tom will protect her from the bad guys chasing after her.

The time has arrived to celebrate Dorothy Powell's life. The local symphony's violinist and celloist Jessica Bailey hired are on the stage playing a classical music piece as family and friends converse quietly, almost reverently, among themselves.

Claire is seated facing her mother's Canasta friends: Lorene, Lizzy Hinson, and Jane Murphy. Jessica and her husband John are a few feet away, talking with Bubba the Barber. As she wanders around the crowd, she listens for anything said about the ossuary.

By 2 p.m. the trash from the luncheon has been collected and placed in metal garbage containers. Ben Perkins and two of his fire-fighting buddies hauled the two cans off in the back of his pickup truck. They will not witness the scattering of Dorothy Powell's ashes in the cow pasture since a shop fire in town has their undivided attention. Clare told them to be careful.

The memorial service begins. Brother Kenny touts all the great things Dorothy Powell has done to help her church and the community. She even helped the police solve tragic murders and single-handedly taken down a serial killer when kidnapped. She is a faithful Methodist, who had lived a good life.

Everyone listens attentively. Lorene can't help but shed a tear. There is so much more to Dorothy Powell than what shows on the surface. She is not only beautiful inside and out, but has been a true friend and advocate for truth and justice.

She just can't be dead! The bad guys can't win!

* * *

"Hold it there!" Tom aims the Magnum semi-automatic revolver at Jim Grossman's head. "We've been expecting you."

Jim slowly turns around, grinning arrows at Tom.

"How did you find out I was coming?"

"Got a call from the rental manager. Paid him double for two more month's rent. You should've paid him more." Tom laughs. "Money talks, or haven't you heard?"

"Look, Tom, I don't have a beef with you."

"If you have a beef with Dorothy, it's with me, too."

"You always were a fool for love."

"I know you were the one who turned Angela. How is Director Carlton? Does he know you're a double-agent?"

"Not anymore, I'm fully dedicated to the U.S. of A."

"Did he send you to kill us?"

"Look, Tom. I'm just doing my job."

"The devil you are, sneaking up on my back porch with a sniper rifle strapped to your side, holding a gun with a silencer."

"Okay, okay . . . I'm putting down my weapon."

"What's going on, Tom?" Dorothy steps out the backdoor.

Fast as quicksand, Jim grabs his mark by the arm and uses her as a human shield. "Sure you want to shoot now, Tom?"

Jim motions to the ladder. "Go down, sweetheart, and you might live to see another day." He follows her down backwards.

Tom's hands are in the air. He won't take a shot at Jim, afraid he'll wound Dorothy. But this game of chase isn't over.

* * *

"Where are we going?" Dorothy asks as the jungle ends and the jeep wheels attack a major paved road. "You won't win."

"Shut up, Dorothy!"

"People like you will go to hell."

He jerks the jeep to the side of the road. The motor idles.

"I can see why Tom likes you."

"But you will never understand love. People like you are incapable of feelings. Money is your god. Go ahead and kill me. I know where I'm going. Besides, my book will be published whether I live or die. I have friends in low places."

Jim absorbs the woman's statement then laughs.

"You are fearless!"

"Double D-D straight, I am!" Dorothy explodes. Her hands and feet are tied so no way she can jump out of the jeep and run.

"All that is very entertaining, but useless prater." Jim pulls out on the road and drives. "I'm in charge of this party, lady."

"Well, at least put on some music!"

"If it will shut you up, no problem."

27

BACK AT ELLIE'S FARM, the memorial service for Dorothy Powell continues in the pasture. A woven basket big enough to carry four is attached by ropes to a balloon filled with helium. Tony is the operator. Claire, June and Billy are his passengers.

People surround the balloon in the afternoon heat, waiting to view the scattering of the deceased ashes.

Different strokes, Tony considers, *for different folks.*

"Will we go up really high, Granny?"

"Not too high," Claire tells June as they climb into the shaky basket attached to the inflated ballon. She heaves a prayer for safety. "Come on, Billy, get in. It's safe, I promise."

"No, Granny! I don't want to! I'm scared."

"Your GG will be proud of you if you do."

"Can she see down from Heaven?" he asks.

"Jesus can!" June calls out. "Com' on Billy, it'll be fun."

"Okay, I guess." He boards and clings to Claire's legs.

"Are we ready to climb?" the operator asks.

"No, no—where are the ashes?" Claire calls out to Lorene.

"Right here!" She hands the ossuary to Claire.

They are not really Dorothy's ashes, just some ash from Ellie's fireplace. But nobody else needs to know that.

The crowd gathered in the grassy field applauds as the balloon ascends some fifty feet. The wind gusts.

"Oh . . ." June and Billy holler as the basket tilts.

"Is it time?" Claire asks Tony.

"You decide. Just scoop out the ashes and toss them overboard," Tony says. "Try not to breathe them."

The wind is brisk and rocks the basket, tilting it. Despite weather opposition, Claire completes her assignment.

Suddenly, the tears roll. If this were really her mother's ashes, she would be saying a final goodbye and the thought is heart-breaking. *Too, too sad.* She bawls harder. Soon to be joined by

June and Billy. The ashes tumble and twist in the rocky atmosphere as the audience erupts with applause.

June cries, "Bye, bye, GG! I love you best of all!"

"Bye, bye, GG!" Billy sobers. "Tell Jesus hi."

Bye, Mama, Claire says to herself, in case she's mistaken and her mother really is dead. Maybe Tom, too. She cries again.

* * *

Back in the Belize jungle, Tom stares at the slashed front tires on his rental truck. Jim made sure he didn't immediately follow the jeep. It's time to call Director Carlton in Langley and bargain for Dorothy's life. Whatever it takes, Tom is willing to do.

Even go to prison.

Dorothy didn't deserve a death sentence at the hands of Jim Grossman when all she had done was act on Tom's behalf. His intent had been noble, though unsanctioned by the CIA. He had only wanted to collect the government's money his first wife Angela had stolen from America and deposited in foreign banks.

And with Dorothy's help, they had succeeded.

But Director Carlton found out he'd held back a million dollars and placed it in a foreign account. Tom had viewed the nest egg as his retirement fund, a gift from the Agency.

Carlton never saw it that way.

They had been happy in Belize. Dorothy even promised to consider marrying him, if they got out of this mess. She forgave him for abandoning her after he'd proposed to her two years ago. She still had his engagement ring, although she wasn't wearing it.

They had kissed goodbye in the grassy field, and Tom had returned to Langley to officially retire. By then, his foreign bank account had been found. He was traded for a more valuable CIA asset who was serving a life sentence in a Moscow, Russia prison.

Tom had barely survived locked up in a dungeon with scant food and water for the next year. When the opportunity came to assist four Serbs in breaking out, he jumped on it. A friend of Tom's had paid off a guard and let them go. Once at the Port of

Moscow, posing as sailors, they had boarded a ship to Miami, Florida. Tom was fluent in the Russian language, a valuable asset to the Serbs. Aboard the ship, he'd emailed Dorothy in Columbia, warning her she was in danger. At that time, he was only guessing.

He'd badly wanted to see her and explain why he'd dropped off the map after he'd proposed. When his feet physically touched Miami soil, he'd phoned the French general he'd met at a pub in Paris, France. Retired from the army, General George Westover had told Tom that his daughter Shelly was recently hired by the CIA as a linguist, speaking fluent English, French, and Spanish.

Dorothy was in Paris with Tom at that time, but he'd never disclosed his meeting with the general. During his Miami call to the general, Tom had explained Dorothy's situation with the CIA, and his need to find out if Director Carlton still viewed her as a threat to the Agency. They knew she was writing a book to expose their unsanctioned activities around the world. However, Tom suspected that Congress had looked the other way.

This is how the clandestine CIA works.

General Westover empathized with Tom's desire to help the woman he loved. He'd spoken to his daughter about obtaining the information Tom wanted. That conversation had occurred seven months ago. Now that they were hiding out in Belize and Director Carlton had sent an agent to abduct Dorothy, Tom was certain her death was eminent if she didn't give him the book.

Tom gathers their necessities with two suitcases from the tree-house and places them in the truck bed. He'd lost valuable time locating a mechanic in the nearest village to purchase two new tires. Another half hour to find the manager and cancel his treehouse rental. He'd told the guy to keep his deposit.

"No one is to be told I was ever here."

"I understand." The manager grinned.

"Thanks for the warning!" He handed him another twenty.

"Will your friend be okay?"

"She'll figure out a way, trust me."

Tom checked the dwelling one more time and climbed in the truck. With a full tank of gas, he was ready to roll to Dorothy.

* * *

By 5 p.m. Saturday, May 29, the memorial service for Dorothy is officially over. All the guests had left Ellie's property but Claire and Lorene. The stage with the speaker lectern, the long serving table, dozens of lawn chairs, and the clothesline with family photographs, had all been taken down and stowed away.

It had been a grueling day. Emotional for all who attended. Claire could almost believe honoring her mother's death was real. The three organizers of the event were exhausted but pleased with how the service had turned out. All would be believers: the guests, the press, those who heard about it through the grapevine, and the Double D-D CIA. Dorothy Jean Powell is deader 'n a doornail.

They sit at Ellie's bar and drink cold sweet tea.

"I worry that someone with the CIA will find Mama."

"Claire, trust your mother. She's smart and capable."

"Thank you, Ellie. But we both know Mama's not skilled in martial arts. How can she defend herself against an assassin?"

"Don't sell your mama short, Claire?" Lorene pipes. "She did it once before. Whoever they send better watch their back!"

Claire glares at Lorene. "What about the book?"

"Trust me, I'll guard her notes like a hawk."

"Good girl!" Ellie raises her glass of tea in a toast. "To Dorothy! For success in publishing her best-selling book! May God bless her and give her a long life!"

Lorene sobers. "Dorothy's already had a long life."

"I need to go home," Claire declares, pooped out.

"You're welcome to spend the night," Ellie offers.

"No, it's time I took charge of my house. Theodore isn't living there anymore. When the divorce is final, I am spending a fortune on redecorating. I want everything that reminds me of him gone. It's time I think about my own future!"

Ellie makes a face at Lorene but doesn't comment.

28

THE TREE-HOUSE CLINT Howard rented for the past seven months was vacant when Agent Joshua Bailey got there. But the residents had not been gone long. Leftover food was in the trashcan under the kitchen sink and some toiletries were in the bathroom. A tube of lipstick, a comb, and a toothbrush.

Thomas Kessler doesn't use pink lipstick.

The manager who rented the tree-house to Clint Howard was as closed-mouthed as a boxer who'd been knocked out. But when Josh had flashed his CIA creds, the guy's mouth dropped open.

"I didn't know he was wanted by the U.S. feds."

"You're not in trouble. I just need to see the place Clint rented. Did you see the woman he was with?" He showed him a recent picture of Dorothy Powell. The guy studied the photo.

"Only at a distance. She had red hair."

"Okay, that's helpful," Josh had said.

"Another guy that knew Clint came by," the manager revealed. "He said he had a wedding gift for the couple."

"Did he show you any credentials?"

"No, but he was an American. Big, like you."

Josh inhaled deeply and thought about it. "A name?"

"No name, but he looked military trained by the way he moved. Scary dark eyes. I didn't mess with 'im."

Had Director Carlton sent someone as backup?

While standing in the living room of the tree-house, Josh assesses what had taken place here. He concludes that the military guy Hosea spoke about had likely been here already and left. No way to determine if Tom and Dorothy had been captured.

Or if they were alive at this juncture. But Josh was not giving up. He steps out on the back porch, then climbs down the ladder.

A number of tire tracks are imprinted in the muddy grass.

A truck, and a smaller vehicle—probably a jeep.

An old wagon sits parked under a tree.

Josh walks around to the front of the house and gets in his rental truck. He calls Jack Carlton on his satellite phone.

It goes straight to voicemail.

He won't leave a message. Jack will see he called. If this is an avoidance tactic, it might mean the agency's favorite crazy assassin has been sent to kill Dorothy, and maybe Tom, too.

He needs to be careful tracking the duo. If Jim Grossman found them, they might already be dead. Either way, the book would not get published, if indeed it has already been written.

* * *

It is dark when Jim Grossman pulls Dorothy out of the back of the Jeep and sets her on her feet. He rips off the gag and orders her to walk. "Where are we?" She can't see a path in front of her.

A flashlight pops on and she realizes they are deep in a wooded area on a crooked mountainous trail.

"Are you going to kill me?" she asks.

Jim huffs and gives her a shove. "Just walk, lady."

"That's not an answer, dumb bunny!"

"Shut up, Dorothy, or the gag goes back on."

"Tom will kill you when he finds us."

Jim gives her another shove and she stumbles a few feet then turns around to face him. "I bet your mother hated you, too."

"I don't have a mother! Keep walking."

"Then that explains it!" She takes a few more steps before jerking around again. "Monsters are born in hell."

Jim cannot help but grin.

"If you're trying to get under my skin, it isn't working."

"Sorry to hear that."

"I have no ethics. My father beat the hell out of me as a kid."

"I'm sorry he did that to you."

"All water under the bridge." Jim despises empathy.

"What should I call you then? My favorite assassin?"

"Call me anything, Dorothy. Doesn't matter."

"No, no, the CIA assassin sent to kill me deserves a name."

"Call me Jim."

"Okay, Jim, where are we going?" Dorothy stumbles along the wooded path with Jim right behind her. She had cramps in her legs from being locked hours in the trunk of the car. She yearns for somewhere safe to sleep. Hopefully, there is a shed, or cabin, at the end of this ascending trail. And she is so . . .thirsty.

Hungry, too. No food since breakfast.

"I worry when you get so quiet," Jim tells Dorothy.

"I was praying for your soul." It is a lie. God should just strike him dead and she would be glad to leave his carcass for the wolves—if there are any in Central America. A bear will do.

After an hour or so, and probably blisters on her feet, Dorothy emerges from the woods. A cabin sits on a hill. Lights are turned on inside. People live there. Hopefully, nice folks.

"Who lives there?" Dorothy points upward.

"You wouldn't know them if I told you."

"Them. A couple? More people like you?"

"As a matter of fact, the parents of a cohort of mine. They are in Witness Protection program."

"What did they do? Blow up something?"

"No, they saved someone I was told to kill. For that, the CIA made it look like they died in an automobile accident."

"Do I need to know all this?" Dorothy mounts the front staircase. There are a dozen steps and her butt is dragging.

"You asked, Dorothy. Just answering."

Jim knocks on the door. An elderly woman with fluffy gray hair stands in the doorway. "Are you lost, young fellow?"

"Sort of . . . we had a wreck and I saw your lights through the woods. Can we come in and make a call? We need help."

Dorothy started to rebuke his statement when Jim pinched her arm hard. She grabbed her forearm and nearly screamed.

"She's hurt and needs medical attention," Jim lies.

The man standing behind the woman is as old as she is. The couple appear to be in their late eighties. Not much older than

Dorothy, so she can't be too critical. They've managed to keep breathing longer than she's likely to . . . unless Tom finds them and takes care of the problem. Now, three people are in danger.

Grace Bailey invites them inside. "Do you work with my son Josh?" she inquires as Dorothy asks to use the bathroom.

"Go with her," Jim tells Grace, and they leave.

"How did you find us?" Gerald Bailey asks the obvious.

"I work for the CIA, and yes, I know Josh. We were in Afghanistan in the early '90s. Sorry you've had to be isolated from your twins for so long. It isn't easy keeping a low profile."

Dorothy opens the bathroom door in time to hear Jim's last sentence. "That's the gospel truth! I tried and failed."

Grace looks hard at Dorothy. "Is this why you're here. Jim is stashing you with us till he finds a safe place for you to land?"

"Something like that," Jim hurriedly says before Dorothy has a chance to answer. "So, can she stay with you a few days?"

Gerald utters, "Sure. We'd love to have her company."

"Thank you." Dorothy means it. Time away from Jim will give Tom more opportunity to track them down.

* * *

Lorene cannot sleep. Saturday was a beautiful day and Dorothy's memorial service honored her highly. But she questions if the book notes in her possession are safe. She now knows for sure that the feds tampered with the ashes—which means they will send someone after the notes. She cannot take a chance they will destroy evidence that Dorothy is the author.

Then there are her letters. Lorene only told the girls about the second letter. The first letter from Dorothy had arrived six weeks after she left Columbia to meet Tom Kessler in Mexico.

In this letter, she had detailed what had taken place while she was overseas with Tom removing millions of U.S. dollars from international banks. Angela Kessler, a double agent for SRV spying on the CIA, had set up the accounts during the early 1990s.

And Tom had convinced Dorothy to withdraw the funds.

CIA Agent James Grossman had murdered Angela. He was also a double agent working on behalf of Russia. Tom had claimed that Angela loved him and was ready to tell Director Carlton the truth. Jim got wind and made sure Angela didn't name him.

That is why there is bad blood between Tom and Jim.

Dorothy's letter had arrived inside a heavy box with the first draft of her book detailing how the CIA drugged her and put her in a mental hospital. Tom had given back the money, but had kept a million for himself. Lorene had told no one what she had.

And she'd never read the contents. Until now . . .

Lorene climbs a flight of stairs to an upstairs bedroom.

Sandwiched between a blanket and stack of sheets in the hall closet sat the box with Dorothy's book. In the event of her death, Lorene had been instructed to take it to her attorney, and ask him to locate a publisher. The deadline was Friday, April 29th.

When word came from Claire that Dorothy's urn with her ashes were due to arrive on that date, Lorene had decided not to rush the book to an attorney. Something seemed amiss.

If Dorothy is alive, there will be more to her story.

Why not get it all? But first, she will read it.

29

IN THE EARLY HOURS of Sunday morning, Dorothy is too pumped to sleep, despite the comfortable mattress on the twin bed. Soon after Jim Grossman had left the house earlier that night on some clandestine mission, she'd taken a shower and devoured a bowel of Grace's delicious vegetable soup. There were toiletries in the bathroom, and a Hawaiian Moo-Moo for Dorothy to wear while Grace washed her dirty clothes. Weary from the day's journey, her stomach full, questions could wait until tomorrow.

Which is actually today.

However, she'd overheard Jim tell Gerald Bailey that he'd be back in a few days, to keep Dorothy there and safe.

Safe is beginning to take on a new tone.

With her captor out of the picture, Dorothy considers telling Gerald about her situation. No. Grace will be more understanding.

But right now, she needs to sleep.

In a drugged state of dreams, hours pass.

A new day dawns. The sun sits high in the sky when Dorothy wakes up in a strange bed and attempts to shake the fog from her memory. Then she recalls yesterday.

Where is Tom?

Hopefully, he'd picked up on their trail.

After a visit to the bathroom, Dorothy patters barefoot into the kitchen and finds Grace making lunch. A whiff of brewing coffee nearly brings her to her knees. The kitchen is roomy with plenty of cabinet space. A square table for four is positioned in front of a bay window overlooking the bushy backyard. This is still the jungle, so she must still be somewhere in Central America.

Dorothy quietly takes in her surroundings.

The temperature gauge on the wall registers 70 degrees Fahrenheit outdoors. The terrain surrounding the house is mountainous. She had traveled a day's journey with Jim from the tree-house she'd shared for the past seven months with Tom.

A glorious time of romance and lots of sexual teasing.

At the base of the mountain, Jim had led the way up a crooked wooded trail to the Bailey's cabin, which took a good forty-five minutes. A place where the Bailey's were placed in the CIA's Witness Protection Program. They had twin sons.

Which made Dorothy wonder if they knew.

"Good morning, Dorothy." Grace says.

"I'm sorry I slept so late." She yawns.

"Well, you needed the rest. Remind me again how you know Josh's friend?" Grace is referring to her eldest twin.

Dorothy tries to decide how much to tell Grace. The woman standing in front of the single sink, with a tea towel thrown over one shoulder and a cup of coffee in hand, looks trustworthy.

"I'm not exactly here by choice, Grace."

"I gathered." Grace nods her head.

"The coffee smells wonderful, may I have a cup?"

"Here, take mine. I haven't taken a sip yet."

Dorothy receives the steamy mug heavy with real cream.

"Thank you, Grace. And especially for the comfortable bed. How much did Jim tell you last night about me?"

"He didn't say much to me, mostly to Gerald." Grace pours herself a mug of brew. "I went to bed soon after you did."

"Where do your boys live?"

"Joshua, the youngest, never stays in one place too long, and I heard that John had moved to a town south of Nashville."

"Which town?"

"Columbia, Tennessee."

Dorothy blinks. *My hometown.*

"Did your source say why John chose Columbia?"

"He actually moved to Nashville first," Grace explains. "Our granddaughter had breast cancer. She died last year."

"I'm so sorry." Dorothy means it. "Did you go to the funeral?" She's suddenly full of unanswered questions.

"No, no, we couldn't. John doesn't even know we're alive." Grace replies as she shoves a pan of cornbread in the oven.

"But Josh does. Why?"

"He's CIA and works for the people who put us here." Grace leans against the cabinet. "Some bad people are looking for us."

I know bad people. Dorothy thinks to herself.

Grace is slender and petite. A spider-web of wrinkles trickle down her thin arms and over her face like a wet mask.

"What is your story, Dorothy?"

"I did something the CIA doesn't like. They sent Jim to make sure I don't talk about it," Dorthy explains. "I need to escape."

"Oh, dear, I don't believe Gerald will agree to that since he promised Agent Grossman he would keep you safe."

"Well, what is your definition of safe, Grace?"

Dorothy privately prays that Lorene followed orders and took her book to Attorney James Sewell to seek a publisher. Once her story is public, she'll have a chance to live a normal life.

* * *

Back in Columbia, Tennessee, Lorene is dressed for the day. She will not phone Dorothy's attorney for an appointment, rather show up with the book, although it still needs editing. There are a lot of typing errors. Dorothy is no professional secretary. And some of the sentences don't make a bit of sense.

But there's enough important facts in the storyline to sufficiently nail the CIA's butt to the whipping post. They would be forced to admit to John Q. Public that they'd committed unpardonable illegal acts against the United States.

A professional editor can finish the book and edit it. It will make a great movie and earn her friend a nice monetary return.

Yet, there is one problem. Lorene groans. Although the published book would vindicate Dorothy and get the CIA off her back, it will incriminate the man she loves, Thomas Kessler.

But that is not Lorene's worry. Tom had used Dorothy to maximize his criminal activity. He's lied to her on numerous occasions. Because of him, she's almost died. And the CIA put her in a mental institution to shut her up. No, watching Agent Tom sweat will be glorious! She'll get the ball rolling.

Sunday School classmates of Dorothy who hadn't made it to the memorial service will likely ask how the goodbye event went.

"Fine," she'll answer. "We said our goodbyes so now she is at rest in the cow pasture where her beloved Arthur had spent so much of his time on earth. I wish you had been there."

No, that didn't sound right.

Oh, well, she'd just wing it. But certainly, keep the crucial information that Dorothy is likely alive out of the conversation. Stick to the facts about the service. Talk about the balloon.

* * *

The closest city to the Bailey's hideaway is Oaxaca, Mexico. With sufficient population and modern conveniences, the area provides an exotic escape for visitors looking to enjoy beautiful terrain and numerous kinds of tours. There is an international airport with direct flights to major cities around the world.

Jim Grossman took no time to tour the area. He has a more important agenda. He is on his way to Nashville, Tennessee, to find the notebook Dorothy claimed she had left behind.

Whoever had the notes would give them over or else . . .

* * *

Meanwhile, Dorothy rests comfortably seated in a swing that overlooks a deep wooded divide behind the Bailey's cabin. Regardless of where Jim has stashed her for a few days, at least she knows it's closer to America than Belize was.

If she could only escape and go home. . .

"Care for more coffee, Dorothy?" Grace asks as she steps out on the back porch. "You've brought us nice weather."

"Is it always this hot in early June?"

"Mid-eighties, usually, and night temperatures range in the mid-sixties. There are open plains where it gets hotter."

"Open plains where?" Dorothy fishes for info.

"You don't know where you are?" Grace asks.

"Grace! Give me a break! Men don't talk."

Grace laughs. "To women, you mean. Gerald is the same way. He never told me why we were put in Witness Protection, only that we weren't safe anymore in America."

Dorothy rolls her eyes. "I wonder if anybody is safe anymore. We live in such a divisive world. Dog eat dog, so to speak."

"I like you, Dorothy. What kind of trouble are you in?"

"I was used by the CIA to remove money from international banks a few years back," she reveals, suddenly trusting Grace.

"Against your will?" Grace sits down in the swing next to her guest. "Were you threatened?"

"No, I was loved into the adventure."

Grace laughs and pushes the swing into motion. "Aren't all of us girls tricked my males? We cave into their wills so quickly."

"I had a choice, Grace. And I do love Thomas Kessler."

"Where have I heard that name before?" Grace's lemony eyes wander over the landscape. "Is he CIA, too?"

"He was, but he quit—it's a complicated story."

"Oh? So, he's part of the reason Jim brought you here. He hasn't decided whose side you are on." Grace wisely concludes.

"He should know by now," Dorothy says, "but staying here with you will give Tom more time to find me."

"Nobody has found us, Dorothy. Except Jim."

"I wrote a book about the CIA's overseas shenanigans, and what they did to me afterwards to shut me up!" Dorothy erupts.

"Whatever you did, Dorothy, is water under the bridge. The CIA is a big organization. You're too small to fight them."

"They drugged me and put me in a damn mental hospital, Grace! If it hadn't been for Tom, I would probably still be there."

"That's terrible, dear. Worse things have happened."

"Espionage, theft, murder—illegal for common folks but not for clandestine government agencies? They are opportunists."

"You won't get an argument out of me, Dorothy."

"I'm not a quitter, Grace. I can't let this go."

"Bad for you, dear. And I don't think Tom will succeed in finding you. If you want to survive, you have to escape."

Dorothy is stunned.

"You'll help me?"

Grace stands up. "Absolutely, I'll help you."

"Will Gerald agree to it?"

"What my husband doesn't know won't hurt him."

Dorothy grins. Grace is trustworthy. She's been used by the CIA, too. And this help is a version of payback.

* * *

Agent Joshua Bailey is a day late and a dollar short, so to speak. All the tire tracks lead north, so that is the way he will go.

If Tom and Dorothy are traveling in a rental car, they will need to stop every couple hundred miles to gas up. Josh has photographs of them he can show station owners. If it were him, he'd leave Mexico by plane. Only major cities in Mexico have international airports. Or, they could find a smaller airport and hire a pilot to take them to a city with an international airport.

Josh needs to determine which route they took. He needs to view a printed map of Mexico and guess where they went. It's a cat and mouse game. Fifty-fifty chances he'd end up failing to catch up with them. Then there is Jim Grossman in the mix.

Josh meditates on a solution.

"If I were Jim, what would be my next move?"

Josh grins.

"I would stash Dorothy somewhere for a couple of days—that is if I hadn't already killed her and disposed of her body."

He rocks his head in thought.

"I'd want to get my hands on the crucial notebook."

Director Carlton had told Josh that Dorothy had written down what she remembered about her time overseas with Thomas Kessler. The notebook was believed to be somewhere in Claire Burkes' house. To cover his bases, Josh would check.

30

JIM GROSSMAN'S PLANE lands at a private airport in Columbia, Tennessee. It is 9:00 a.m., Monday morning. He's tired from the long trip, but has a job to do. He'd searched Claire Burke's Brentwood house in Nashville for Dorothy's notebook yesterday while she was away at church. The security system wasn't even on.

As he deplaned with only a small bag, he laughs.

Claire had even left a window unlocked in the laundry room. Homeowners can be so lax with protecting their assets.

And I know all the tricks.

Jim's next stop is at Lorene Perkins' house. It appears that Dorothy's neighbor for decades is her closest confidante. If anyone has the notebook, or a copy of the manuscript detailing the inner workings of the CIA, it will be Lorene. But he soon discovers the elderly woman is more cautious than Claire.

Jim jiggles with the front door lock and gets into the foyer. He hears beeping. The security system is working. That means the home owner is probably not home. But if he can type in the code and shut it off, the police department will not be alerted to a break-in. He will have plenty of time to search the house.

The beeping is insistent as he finds the control panel.

Here goes . . . he studies the digits.

He has Lorene's birthdate, as well as her deceased husband's. Both of their social-security numbers, even their daughter Heather's birthdate. A whole list of number possibilities a page long. Homeowners usually select codes easy to remember.

Jim first tries Crawford Perkin's birthdate. Nope. The first four digits of his social gets the green light on the security panel. Now for a thorough search where no one will think to look.

* * *

It's noon on Monday and Attorney Jacob Dunwoody has the door to his office shut. He doesn't want to be disturbed. Now in his early sixties, he would rather retire. But his wife is an avid shopper, so he still represents a few clients that had used him to financially settle their ugly divorces, or file legal papers with Maury County involving their wills or trusts. He suffers a pain in his lower back. Dadgum stenosis spurred by osteoarthritis.

Jacob gulps down two Tylenol. He coughs as he exhales cigar smoke. Joann forbids him to smoke in the house. You'd think his third wife would give him a break since he denies her nothing.

The intercom system buzzes, interrupting Jacob's reverie.

My secretary. He doesn't want to be bothered.

Another buzz. Jacob crushes out the butt of his cigar and groans as he picks up his phone. "What is it, Tisha?"

He stares at the ash glowing red in the glass tray.

"Lorene Perkins is here to see you, Jacob."

"Do I have an appointment?" He peruses the large pad on his desk with a calendar of days, weeks, and months printed on it.

"She says not," Tisha replies. "But claims it's urgent."

"Isn't it always?" He sighs. "Send her in."

He opens the door for her.

"Hello, Lorene, how are you?"

"I'm fine, and our meeting has nothing to do with me."

"Okay . . ." wrinkles gather on his forehead. "Then how may I help who you represent on this first day of a new week?"

Lorene makes firm eye contact.

"Here! *This!*" She plops Dorothy's manuscript on top of Jacob's desk calendar. It's a three-hundred-page, hand-written book, difficult to read, but at least he has it now and she doesn't.

"What is this, Lorene?" He turns the thick envelope over to study the back. "And why are you giving *this* to me?"

"It's Dorothy Powell's book," she replies.

"I heard she died." He carefully removes the pages from the thick envelope and reads the title of the book on the front page.

"CIA Shenanigans?" His eyes bug out.

"Dorothy mailed the book months ago with a letter instructing me to give it to you if she wasn't back in Columbia by April 29." Lorene pauses. "That date is long past, so here it is."

Jacob scratches his neck, puzzled.

"So, Dorothy wrote about the CIA and how they operate." He motions for Lorene to take a seat in front of his desk as he uncomfortably drops into his chair. *Hemorrhoids.*

Jacob groans, his strained gray eyes revealing poor health.

"I heard Dorothy's memorial service was on Saturday at Ellie Perkins' farm. I'm so sorry. Do you know how she died?"

"About that—appearances can be deceiving. There are questions surrounding her ashes—which makes me wonder."

"If she's really dead?" Jacob nods his head.

"My friends and I believe the ashes aren't Dorothy's."

"Then why have a memorial service?"

"An act of faith to make people believe Dorothy is dead. Including the corrupt CIA, who despises her."

Jacob chuckles. "I heard there was even a balloon."

"Oh, yes! If Dorothy is dead, she will be so proud."

"I see, so why are you involving me?" Jacob queries.

"To make sure her notebook and manuscript are safe," Lorene explains. "Dorothy trusts you to find a publisher."

"I'm not a book agent, Lorene!"

"No, but you can time-stamp the book and notes into evidence that can later be used in a court of law."

"Oh, I don't know. Fooling with the CIA is dangerous."

"Tell me about it, Jacob. You do this for Dorothy, and you can try the court case if it comes to that." Lorene embellishes her offer. "Dorothy said she'd pay you a percent of her sales. If the book is successful, you'll get rich in the process. Please help her."

Jacob shakes his head. "That could get me killed, Lorene."

"Don't tell me you're afraid of the federal government?"

"Damn straight, I am. And I don't even play Poker."

* * *

Jim Grossman is finished searching Lorene Perkin's house by noon. The book isn't here. He walks into the foyer and resets the security system, then drives away in a Tesla he'd rented at the Nashville airport. Why not travel elegantly at the Gov's expense?

* * *

Events are unfolding on many levels. With the help of Grace Bailey, Dorothy Powell has devised a plan of escape from the clutches of Agent James Grossman. Her exit from the house will take place during the wee hours of Tuesday morning, long after Grace's husband Gerald is snoring in his bed. One thing Dorothy knows if she's to live, she must find Tom. He'll know what to do.

* * *

Meanwhile, Jim is on his way to an address located in the Columbia Country Club. Gerald and Grace Bailey's son John lives there with his wife Jessica. He doesn't know if she will remember meeting him at a going-away party in D.C. during the early 1990s, but John certainly will. Hopefully, he'll learn more from them.

* * *

Thomas Kessler is in Oaxaca, Mexico, at the international airport, talking to one of the managers. He identifies himself as an American federal agent then shows the guy a picture taken at an office party in D.C. during the early 1970s. All the major players in the CIA spy-game are shown in the printed photograph.

Tom is pleased when the guy points to James Grossman.

"Him. He bought a ticket to Nashville, Tennessee on Saturday," the manager reports. "Is he CIA, like you?"

"Yes," Tom lies. He no longer works for the Agency. Although his efforts to rectify Angela's misdeeds, Director Carlton had never seen it that way. Jack had sent him to a Russian prison. Worse, he'd sent an assassin to kill Dorothy.

He had to protect her since no one else could.

31

GPS LOCATES THE address Jim is searching for in the Country Club for John and Jessica Bailey. Fairly newcomers to Tennessee, over a year ago their only daughter in Nashville died from breast cancer. Jim cannot fathom why Josh's brother lives in a country town like Columbia when Atlanta has so much more to offer in amenities. Possibly, he is here at Josh's request. But purchasing an expensive house to keep up appearances seems overboard.

However, if John is spying on Dorothy Powell's friends, his wife is probably helping him. Jim needs to know what they've found out so he can proceed and locate Dorothy's notebook.

He taps on the Bailey's front door.

Chimes go off as he waits. A lovely woman in her mid-sixties opens up to Jim. He smiles. "I presume you are Jessica Bailey?"

She twists her moist pink lips to one side of her mouth.

"You must have the wrong address." Her golden-brown eyes look him over. "I've never seen you before. If you're selling—"

"I'm not a salesman. I'm here on behalf of John's brother," Jim quickly says, anticipating the door about to slam in his face.

"You know Joshua?"

"Oh, yes, for decades now." He removes his CIA cred and shows them to her. "If I may come in, I'll explain why I'm here."

"So, Agent Grossman, you're here to see John about his brother?" Jess stands guard the entry to protect her turf.

"Yes, it's important, Mrs. Bailey." He tries to look humble.

"Wait here." Jessica closes the door.

Jim hears a click. The lock. He grins.

She doesn't trust me. Smart lady.

Jim waits. The door opens again. A man stands there.

"I'm John Bailey, Agent Grossman. What about Josh?"

"May I come in, John? It's getting hot out here."

The door swings wide as John motions with his hand for his visitor to step indoors. "You better be legit."

"I am," Jim says. "Thank you for your time."
Never hurts to not bite the hand you hope will feed you.
"You landed well." Jim compliments the property.

The house is impressive, wood floors throughout, expensive furniture and artwork on the walls. The décor is splendid.

"Let's sit in the den and talk," John suggests.

Jim follows, taking in his surroundings, always looking for exits in case the conversation turns nasty.

"Jess?" John calls out. "Will you get us a glass of tea?"

"Sure," she calls back from the kitchen.

John sits on the sofa, hands on both knees, staring at his visitor. "Is my brother in trouble?"

"No, but he sent me because he's out of the country on an assignment," Jim reveals, True, except for sending him.

"What kind of assignment?"

"He's looking for Dorothy Powell."

John chuckles.

"What' so humorous?"

"You can send word for Josh to stop looking. Dorothy's ashes were scattered over the pasture of the farm she used to own. Jess and I attended her memorial service this past Saturday."

"Last time I saw her, she was still breathing," Jim says.

"Well, then, problem solved. Tell that to her daughter, Claire Burkes. I'm sure the news will greatly relieve her grief."

"Not yet, John. First, I need to find Dorothy's notebook."

"I don't know anything about a notebook," John says.

"It's like a diary. It contains information about the Agency that is classified. Sensitive facts that can damage the CIA's image and compromise American interests worldwide."

Jim pauses for John to evaluate his statement.

"How do you know about this notebook, Agent Grossman.?"

"Know what?" Jess enters the den with two tall plastic tumblers with ice tea, handing one to John and one to their guest.

"Can we keep this between us, John?" Jim asks.

"Thanks, Mrs. Bailey."

"Jess, please," she says and lingers.

"Sorry, honey, this conversation is not for your ears."

"Why not? Is Josh in danger?"

"Leave us, honey. We can talk about this later."

Honey? Give me a break.

As soon as Jessica is out of earshot, Jim says, "Now that's what a good wife is all about. You're a lucky guy, John."

"We have a good marriage, but that's none of your business."

"No harm intended," Jim apologizes. "I need your help, John. You know people in Columbia can discreetly ask questions I can't. I need to know if Dorothy has finished her book."

"To determine how much harm it poses to the Agency."

"Exactly!"

"Look, Jim, I'm already snooping for Josh. If you know him as well as you say, you ought to know that."

"Let's just say Josh and I have different assignments where Dorothy Powell is concerned, and leave it at that," Jim states. "There are certain facts you're better off not knowing."

Jim pauses to take a long draw from his glass of cold tea.

"And what exactly is the CIA's end game?" John inquires.

"Find the damn notebook and destroy it!"

"I see . . ." John says.

"If there's a completed book, I need to destroy it. Then the CIA will negotiate with Dorothy for a ceasefire—so to speak."

"How nice of them!" John facetiously remarks.

"Upon agreement, she can return home and resume a dull existence for the rest of her life—which can't be all that long at eighty-six." Jim stares at the homeowner. "Will you help me?"

"And Josh asked you to ask me to help you?"

"Scout's Honor." Jim signs, never a Scout.

* * *

Agent James Grossman had been gone for ten minutes when Jess reappeared in the den, one hand sassily parked on a hip.

What was that all about, John? Did he threaten you? What's his business with us? And why do you look so distraught?"

John pats the sofa. "Come sit by me, honey."

"This can't be good news."

Carrying a platter of chicken-salad sandwiches and a bowl of salty potato chips in her hands, Jess sets both on the glass-top table in front of the sofa. "I thought we'd make lunch easy."

"Fine with me. I'm hungry after an early round of golf this morning." He nabs a sandwich and washes it down with cold tea.

"Quit eating and tell me what the agent said."

"He asks for my help." John nabs another sandwich and gulps tea to wash it down. "I didn't realize how hungry I was."

"Slow down, you'll get choked," Jess warns, yet to begin eating her lunch. If Agent Grossman is telling the truth, and Josh sent him to ask John for help, there may be danger ahead.

"Do you trust Agent Grossman?" Jess looks hard at John.

"He claims Dorothy Powell is alive. The book she wrote about the CIA will harm American interests around the world. There's also a missing notebook. He needs to find both."

"Did he offer proof she's alive and the book exists?"

"No, he did not," John replies. "And we both know CIA agents lie, don't we?" He mulls over Grossman's request.

"What did he specifically ask you to do, John?"

"He wants me to talk to Dorothy's friends."

"You mean spy on them, like we're already doing." Jess shakes her head. "Do you believe him?"

"I don't know, Jess. But I would also like to know if such a book exists. If we can locate it before Agent Grossman, we'll give it to Josh. He'll know the proper way to handle it. I certainly don't want to be responsible for hurting Dorothy Powell."

"What do you mean??

"Grossman claims if the CIA destroys the book, Dorothy can come home and live the rest of her days in peace."

"But you don't believe that."

32

Tuesday, June 1

CIA AGENT JOSHUA BAILEY had visited every rental agency in Oaxaca, Mexico. He didn't believe that Jim Grossman would fly with Dorothy back to the states. He'd stashed her somewhere safe until he returned. That meant Dorothy was still breathing.

I have to find her before Jim returns.

Josh had spent Monday night in the city, reviewing all the information on rentals provided by several agencies. He'd decided on the three best locations to see in person. Early Tuesday, he'd located the first two. Young couples occupied those residences.

He is on his way to a third location in the mountains east of the city. An elderly couple had rented the house two years ago and the manager considered them permanent residents. Jim probably knows the people in order to trust Dorothy in their care.

That means they have a connection to the CIA.

Everything spelled Witness Protection. Someone who had been previously involved with CIA business and needed to hide from an enemy. This mountainous location felt like someplace he'd find Dorothy. But there is no easy approach to the property.

Josh pulls his rental car into a parking area off the main road. Multiple tire and foot tracks are pressed into the dirt. There's a path leading away from the road, so he'll walk the rest of the way to the residence. Forty minutes later, he stands at the edge of a clearing. The cabin on the hill is impressive from this distance.

The structure features front and back porches with exotic views of the surrounding mountainous terrain. Josh stealthily approaches from the front, and climbs steps to the front porch.

He listens for sounds inside.

Late sleepers, or they have detection devices in the woods.

No way to determine who was inside except knock.

***

Lorene left Attorney Jacob Dunwoody's office on Monday after witnessing him lock Dorothy's hand-written manuscript in his office safe. Jacob knew important people in Nashville who could get her book to a reputable publisher. Releasing the story to the public might save Dorothy's life. Unless, the feds enjoy killing.

It's Tuesday morning and she's on her way over to Jane's when her cell phone dings. "Yes?"

"It's me, Claire. I need to see you, Lorene."

"Sure. Where are you?"

"Home. I can't stay here any longer by myself. It's driving me crazy waiting for my divorce with Ted to be final. I need to get out of Nashville. My mother said you were a good listener."

Lorene thought she heard Claire weeping quietly.

"Of course, you need a change, dear. I have one errand to run then I'll meet you at Bart's for lunch. 12:30, okay?"

"Sounds good. I'll be there earlier, but I also have some things I need to do." Claire does not reveal she is considering selling her house in Brentwood and moving to Columbia.

"I'll see you at Bart's." Lorene ends the call.

Jane is not home. No hair appointment on Tuesday, Lorene presumes she's puttering around in her backyard garden.

She rounds the side of the house and spies the shirttail of her friend wagging in the morning breeze like a puppy dog's.

"Jane!" she calls out, not to startle her.

The gray head pops up as she struggles to stand.

"Lorene! Was I expecting you?"

"Always expect a surprise, Jane, and you'll never be disappointed." She watches as her friend puts her spade in the bucket then pulls off her garden gloves. "I'm coming!"

They enter the house through the backdoor. Jane washes her hands and face in the bathroom then returns to the kitchen. She finds Lorene pilfering through her fridge. "Don't you have any sodas? I'm thirsty," Lorene calls out. "You need to shop."

"I will, Lorene. On Wednesday, when the new Kroger ads come out. Why are you here?" She fixes two tall glasses of ice water and hands one to Lorene. "Here, thirsty camel!"

Lorene heartily drinks. "Thanks, I was thirsty."

"Let's sit a spell, I'm worn out."

"You're too old to keep a flower garden, Jane," Lorene says as they enter the den and find seats. "Hire someone younger."

Jane frowns, inhales. "I don't have any relatives I can call on like you do, Lorene. And my money is not unlimited."

"Sorry, friend. I'm just worried about you."

"I know—so why have you stopped by this early?"

Lorene plops her butt in the recliner and kicks back. "This chair reminds me of Crawford. When he was around, I didn't have to think about everything by myself. And now I have to think about Dorothy, too, and what is best for her."

Jane grins.

"What?"

"What did Dorothy do now?" Jane snickers.

"Well, she didn't come home like she promised," Lorene fusses. "And she unloaded a big responsibility on my shoulders."

"What kind of responsibility?"

"Well, her book. But I've taken care of that."

Jane leans forward on the sofa. "What do you mean?"

"I didn't tell you that Dorothy finished the book last year. I did not know myself until I received a UPS copy a couple months after she left Columbia. She said Thomas Kessler was with her."

"So . . . the book?" Jane glares.

"Yesterday, I gave it to Attorney Jacob Dunwoody. He's been handling Dorothy's legal affairs for decades."

"And what is he going to do with it?"

"Dorothy included a letter with the book, instructing me to give it to her attorney if she wasn't back in Columbia by the last Friday in April. She wants him to find a publisher for her."

"She must trust Jacob with her life." Jane nods.

"Yes, she does. He was also Arthur's good friend."

"Okay . . ." Jane's gaze strays, "so, if the book is so important, why haven't you taken it to Jacob before now?"

"Well . . ." Lorene shakes her head, "I don't know. The timing just didn't feel right. I kept thinking Dorothy would come home and take her own book to a publisher. But now . . ."

"Now that she might really be dead, you have."

"Yes." Tears glaze her eyes at the idea.

"Have you told Lizzy any of this?" Jane asks.

Lorene shakes her head no.

"Okay, let's go over to her house and tell her together. She'll be upset that you think Dorothy is dead," Jane says. "First, I need to change clothes. I won't be long, watch something on TV."

33

IN THE MOUNTAINS OF Mexico, Josh Bailey knocks on the cabin door and anxiously awaits a response.

If Dorothy is here, there's a lot more to the story than he sees.

The realtor said an elderly couple rented the cabin two years ago. If they took Dorothy in on behalf of Jim Grossman, they must be somehow connected to the CIA. It's the only thing that would make sense. He hears the door lock turn then the door opens. A familiar face stands before Josh. "Mom?"

"Josh!" She glances at the front yard. "Did anyone see you come here?" She pulls her twin son inside the cabin.

"Mom?" Josh stands dazed, gazing in unbelief. "They told us you and Dad died in an automobile accident two years ago."

"No, we didn't, son. They told us to lie."

"The CIA." He nods. He had it all wrong.

Gerald Bailey walks over to his son and hugs him.

"I'm sorry, Josh. They said not to tell you or your brother we were alive," Gerald explains. "We witnessed a murder at a mall committed by a Russian assassin. The SRV put out a murder contract on us." He pauses. "Please don't be mad at us."

Josh spurts, "But I saw your bodies at the morgue in Atlanta. John and I identified you. We arranged for your funerals. We cried when they put your caskets in the grave." He felt faint.

"Sit down, Josh," Grace orders. "You look weary to the bone. I'll get you a glass of water." She starts for the kitchen.

"No, Grace, get him a Bourbon and Coke, he needs it," Gerald pipes from the foyer. "Let's go into the den, son."

After a strong swallow of alcohol, Josh asks the question he came to ask. "Did an agent named Jim Grossman come here?"

"Yes, he said he knew you," Grace says.

"We worked together, but his job differs from mine."

"In what way, son?" Gerald asks.

"He's an assassin for the CIA. I'm an investigator."

"Does this have anything to do with Dorothy Powell?" Grace asks, worry lines on her forehead. "He asked us to watch her."

Josh half stands, "Is she here now?"

"No." Gerald shakes his head. "Your mother helped her escape. She left the cabin early this morning before I woke up."

"Which direction did she go?"

"You can't leave this late in the day, Josh," Grace says. "It's not safe in the woods. Spend the night then you can try and find Dorothy tomorrow. What did she do so terrible?"

"She told the truth about the CIA," Josh answers.

Gerald laughs. "Well, that is a problem."

* * *

As night fell on Tuesday, Dorothy walked up to a house and knocked on the front door. A young woman opened up.

"Hi, my name is Dorothy Powell. I need help."

"Diago!" she calls back. "A woman's here to see you."

Dorothy waits on the doorstep, shivering. Instead of going down the mountain, she went up, thinking any sensible person escaping captivity would have gone down to a town or city and asked for help. Well, she wasn't an ordinary sensible person.

"Who are you?" Diago asks in broken English.

"I'm an American. I need to borrow your phone."

Diago looks at the young woman. "What 'd ya think?"

"Let her use the phone," Maria says.

"Thank you." Dorothy steps inside the house and walks over to the fireplace where a roaring fire is in progress. "Is it always this cold high up in Mexico?" She bends over to warm her cold hands.

"It's hot during middays," Maria answers. "Would you like something hot to drink?" Her English is much better.

"Did you walk here?" Diago asks.

"Yes. It's a complicated story. I've sort of been lost from my, uh, husband. We got separated a few days ago," Dorothy explains, not ready to disclose too much. She doesn't know them.

"Here. Hot cider," Maria announces and hands Dorothy a mug. "I have muffins if you'd like one with your beverage."

"I would." Dorothy sips the delicious cider. "You speak well, Maria. Are you originally from Mexico?"

"No, Italy. I met Diago on a Caribbean cruise. He won the three-day cruise for selling the most—what is it you sell, honey?" Maria asks him. "Never mind, we hit it off." Maria shows Dorothy the diamond ring on her third finger of her left hand.

"That is beautiful, Maria, congratulations! How long have you and Diago been married?" It saddens Dorothy to think that she had to leave her engagement ring from Tom at Claire's house. It is hidden at the top of a storage cabinet in the laundry room.

"Four months. We're just renting," Diago answers.

Dorothy looks between the two newlyweds.

"Mind if I make my call now?"

* * *

If Tom were Jim, he would stash Dorothy in a safe location with someone associated with the Agency. Hoping to gain more information, he phones Langley on his SAT phone and asks to speak to Director Carlton. He identifies himself and waits.

"Yeah, Tom. I understand you've been a naughty boy!"

Chuckling, he says, "Dorothy doesn't deserve the treatment you CIA boys have been dishing out. If you had only trusted me, I could have taken care of this problem for you." He'd promised to locate Dorothy's original manuscript and bury it for the CIA.

"So, you're calling to say you have the book?"

"I don't. Why did you send Jim Grossman?"

"In case you fail to turn over the evidence," Jack replies.

"I haven't failed, Jack, I need more time," Tom says.

"I'd quit looking for her. Jim's handling things."

He senses the Director smiling.

"Did you instruct him to kill her?" Tom asks.

"No, I just said to take care of the problem."

"Well, I hope he hasn't done that."

"Dorothy is dangerous," Jack says.

"Jim doesn't have his act together," Tom says. "Otherwise, why did he fly alone to America on Sunday?" He hears Jack breathing hard. "Is she still in Central America?"

Tom needs usable intel.

"Like I said, Jim's on it, so quit looking."

"I can't do that." Tom waits a beat. "But I will find Dorothy. If she won't give up the book . . ." He leaves much unsaid.

"You're willing to take care of our problem?"

"If it would square things with you," Tom says. "I don't see myself running for the rest of my days." He pauses. "And if you want the million back that I stole, we can talk about it. No good to me if I'm dead." He negotiates for an edge. "But I need info."

"What kind of information?"

"Do you have safe houses in Mexico?"

"Is that where you are?" Jack asks.

"At the moment. I need to verify if Dorothy is deceased."

"Well," the Director quips, "her family sure thinks so. They scattered her ashes not long ago over a cow pasture."

"So, I heard . . ." Tom mouths. "The safehouses?"

"There are three." Carlton gives the GPS coordinates.

Only one is within driving distance from Oaxaca, Mexico.

* * *

Lorene had dropped Jane off at her house around 3 p.m. after they had lunch with Lizzy. She shared taking Dorothy's book to Attorney Jacob Dunwoody for safekeeping. Lizzy agreed with Jane it was the right thing to do. Home now, she is exhausted.

Her cell phone dings.

"Not now!" she calls out to the device on her breakfast bar. "I'm taking a break from thinking." It's a conversation with herself since the phone can't talk back. Then she hears the message unspooling . . . *Lorene, it's me, Dorothy.*

As fast as a cat after meow, Lorene races to the bar and grabs the phone. "Dorothy! Are you alive?"

"Of course, I am, dumb bunny, why else would I call?"

"Where are you?"

"Mexico, somewhere in the mountains," Dorothy replies.

"Is Tom with you?"

"No, I was kidnapped by a CIA assassin."

Lorene places her hand over the phone and whispers, "Is your captor with you now?" She's trembling over the idea.

"Double D-D no! If he was with me, Lorene, I would not be calling you," Dorothy fusses. "I need a ride to the airport."

"Uh, sure. Give me the address." Lorene scrambles for a notepad and pen. "I'm ready. Where are you?"

"What's the address here?" Dorothy asks.

"Who are you talking to?" Lorene asks.

"The couple renting this cabin," she replies. "Their address is a post office box address in a city called Oaxaca."

"Would you spell that?"

"Look it up on the map, Lorene, I'm kind'a short of time here. I have a killer on my coattail and I need to escape this godforsaken country and come home, and . . ." Dorothy rambles on.

"Okay, okay, calm down, dear. You should know I took your book to Attorney Jacob Dunwoody's on Monday. He locked it in his safe." Lorene looks for Oaxaca, Mexico on a world globe.

"I don't have a cell phone, Lorene, so I'll have to call you back when you arrange a ride for me. I trust you."

"Oh, that's so sweet, Dorothy. You had a beautiful memorial service at Ellie's farm. More than forty people came to say goodbye to you—you should be so pleased. Your Methodist pastor said wonderful things about you. It was so sad seeing your ashes scattered over Arthur's cow pasture—"

"Stop it, Lorene! I'm not dead. Help me out here. Meanwhile, I'm going to try and make it back to the city another way."

"Okay, okay, I'll see what I can do."

"Good. I'll call you back tomorrow morning."

"Take care, okay?"

34

JOSH SPENT TUESDAY night with his parents. Wednesday came on with a flurry of storms. Rain poured down on the cabin like a drunk man dumping kegs of beer on the rooftop.

"Good morning, son."

"Mornin', Mom." Josh yawns. "Something smells good." He peeks into the boiling pot. "Vegetable soup?"

"Yes, for our lunch." She continues to dice onions and carrots while the beef chunks stew in the big aluminum pot.

"I can't stay for lunch, Mom. I need to find Dorothy."

Grace faces her son, her hips hitched on the edge of the kitchen counter. "I like Dorothy. Why can't the CIA just let her be? She said her book is fiction based on a true story."

"It's the true part that worries the CIA," Josh says. "I need to get my hands on the book and read it. Maybe I can negotiate a truce between Director Carlton and Dorothy. If no real person is named in the book, and the locations are changed, maybe . . ."

"And maybe if she won't agree?" Grace inquires.

"It's not my call, Mom. I'm reasonably sure the agent who brought Dorothy here intends to kill her when he returns."

"Good luck with that! She's long gone, son."

"How far can she get on foot in these mountains?" Josh splays his hands. "Look out the window! It's raining cats and dogs. Weather forecast says it won't stop for twenty-four hours."

Grace smiles. "My point exactly, Josh. No use you running off looking for Dorothy today. It's been two years since your dad and I spent time with you. Let's make this visit count."

"We should call John," he suggests.

"We were told not to; it would put us in danger."

"I can use my encrypted cell phone. No one will know."

"Okay, but first let's wake up your daddy and have breakfast. Then we'll all talk to John." She removes the bacon and eggs from the fridge. "Well, go and wake up your daddy!" Grace orders.

***

Dorothy hangs up the landline and looks at her two new friends. "That was my best friend in America. She's going to work out a ride for me to the airport, I need to leave the country."

"Are you in trouble?"

"I was separated from my friend," Dorothy replies.

"Roads are too muddy to travel today," Diago says.

"We really would like to help, Dorothy, but Diago is right. There will be mudslides. Too dangerous to travel today."

Dorothy didn't like the answer, but said she understood, then added, "Okay, if my friend can't get a ride for me, will you drive me to Oaxaca? I will send you money when I get home."

Diago looks longingly at Maria.

"I know, I know, I'm a stranger, but I keep my promises." She removes a locket Tom gave her for her birthday. "Here."

"Is it gold?" Diago asks, examining the jewelry.

"Yes." She hoped Tom hadn't stolen it.

Maria examines the locket, too. There are two pictures inside: one of Dorothy and one of Tom. "Who is this man?"

"Tom. I'm engaged to him. He saved my life."

Diago scratches his head. "And now you want us to help save your life." It's not a question. It's a risky proposition.

"I'm publishing a book about the American CIA soon. I will be paid a lot of money, Diago. I promise to pay you."

Maria touches his arm. "I think we should trust Dorothy."

His answer was in Spanish, too quick to understand.

"Okay, tomorrow. We'll take my old truck," he agrees.

***

As promised, Grace's soup was superb. Josh could tell his daddy wasn't feeling well. "What's wrong, Dad? Are you sick?"

"Son, I'm always sick. I'm eighty-eight years old. My feet have traveled many a mile." He fondly looks at his son. "Don't worry about me. Your mom and I have lived our lives. Live yours."

They sat in the living room together as Josh called John's residence. The landline's message center came on. He ended the call. "I can't leave a message, Mom. We'll call back later."

* * *

Ten minutes later, Jessica Bailey saw the landline blinking. She listened for a message and heard only breathing.

Who called? Friend or foe?

John had left thirty minutes ago for Columbia to purchase some golfing supplies at a hometown merchant store. While waiting for him to return, she read a novel. When his SUV pulled into the garage and he didn't come inside, she went out to the garage and found him unloading his supplies in the cabinet.

"What is it, Jess? You look stressed?"

"We got a silent call earlier. Should I be worried?"

"Probably a wrong number," he says, and walks to the fridge where he removes a bottle of Bud. "Want a cold beer?"

"No, thanks." Jess ponders the call.

"Okay, okay, honey, exactly what is it about the silent call that bothers you?" He follows her inside the house and sits at the bar.

"Ever since Josh asked you spy on Dorothy's friends, I've had no peace. What do you know about Agent Jim Grossman?"

John swivels toward Jess. "You worry he's spying on us?"

"All we know about him is what he told us," Jess says. "He claims to be a friend of Josh's. Why is he looking for Dorothy?"

"You think it's about the book she wrote." John scrutinizes his wife. "It won't see the light of day if the CIA has anything to do with it. The last thing they want is to be publicly humiliated. Besides, how many people around the world will be hurt by the truth? The Agency is America's ears and eyes around the world."

"Does that give them the right to harass Dorothy?"

"Honey, we know freedom of speech is a myth."

"Well, I don't trust Agent Grossman or Josh." She considers telling him about how Josh raped her soon after they married. The awful part of that story was the result. Rita wasn't John's daughter.

"He's my flesh and blood, Jess. I love my brother."

"Would you still, if I told you what he's really like?"

"What's that supposed to mean?" John snags a cookie from the jar. "I don't understand why you hate Josh so much."

"Because he raped me, John!"

A snarl first that morphs into a grin. "You slept with Josh first, or have you forgotten?" The conversation turns nasty.

"Only because you swapped places on our third date!" Jess's voice heightens. "I'm talking about later."

John wags his head. "Later, when?"

"After we were married. You were at the office when Josh stopped by the apartment. He forced me to have sex with him."

"For God's sake, Jess, that was decades ago! Can't you let it go? Josh is Josh. And you are no less a noble woman."

Jess could not withhold her tears.

"There's more, John."

That has his attention.

"Rita is Josh's daughter, not yours."

"What?"

"You heard me, John."

"Does Josh know?" He's shaking Jess hard.

"Stop it, John, you're hurting me!"

She is shocked when he slaps her hard.

"You're a lying piece of shit!" he screams.

Jess rubs her stinging cheek.

"Oh, I see now whose side you're on!" she hisses, grabs her purse, and walks toward the door leading to the garage.

"Where are you going, Jess?" John calls after her.

"I'm not sure." She slams the door behind her. Seconds later, she pulls out of the driveway, tears plummeting down her cheeks.

35

JESSICA BAILEY SITS in her BMW in Lorene's driveway. She realizes the only true friends she has in Columbia are the girls she plays Canasta with every Friday afternoon. They share burdens with one another and care about how life unfolds.

She opens the door and mounts the porch. She has been driving around town for over and hour before deciding to come see Lorene Perkins. She needs to talk to a friend about her situation with John. She needs to cry on somebody's shoulder.

The door opens before Jess knocks.

"What are you doing here this late?"

Jess hardly realized that darkness had wrapped its inky hands around her. "I, uh, I had a fight with John, and—"

"No need to explain, girlfriend, come on in. You've come to the right place. This is Heartbreak Hotel for women who get their feelings hurt," Lorene babbles on as she pulls Jess inside.

"I'm sorry to interrupt your evening," Jess says. "But I did not have any place else to go." She is visibly shaking.

"Come in the kitchen, dear, and I'll make you a hot drink."

"Thank you, Lorene."

Jess walks through the hall and enters the den/kitchen combo. The house smells like roast beef, and she's suddenly hungry. "Have you eaten already?" she asks Lorene.

"Yes, but I have plenty of leftovers—roast beef with potatoes and carrots, and a green-bean casserole. The perfect meal for someone in need of a boost in morale. Let me make you a plate."

Jess smiles. "You don't have to ask twice."

The food was the best she had tasted, probably because someone else had prepared it. When Jess had cleaned her plate, she sat back in the dining room chair and sighed.

"Better?" Lorene was seated across the table from her, observing her every expression. "Now, for a cup of coffee."

"Decaf, please." Jess wilts from a full stomach.

"Coming up." Lorene fixes two cups.

After the girls had finished a slice of pecan pie with ice-cream and two cups of decaf coffee, Lorene led the way into the den.

"You sit in Crawford's recliner, Jess. It's the more anointed chair I have in my house. I swear I have confessed so many sins to God in that chair, He might just let me bring it into Heaven."

Jess can't help but chuckle. "You sure know how to treat a guest like royalty." She is able to relax for the first time since she admitted to John that Rita was his brother's daughter.

"Now, you just tell me what's on your mind, Jess," Lorene opens the door to a serious discussion. "And after you tell me, if you don't feel comfortable about going home, you'll stay the night in my guest bedroom. Okay?" She sits on the sofa and clutches a throw pillow, preparing to hear something terrible.

"I haven't been totally honest with you and the girls," Jess begins. "John and I have been spying on you."

Lorene swallows hard. "Come again?"

"John's brother is a CIA agent and asked him to move to Columbia to spy on Dorothy Powell's friends," Jess continues.

"Does John always do what his brother asks?"

"Yes, and he also insisted that I wiggle my way into your lives so I could also gather information." Jess stops. "I'm sorry."

Lorene tries to digest the news.

"So . . . why are you telling me this now?"

"I told John I would not spy on my friends anymore, that I didn't care what his brother wanted," Jess confesses. "But that isn't why I came here. I was so angry with John I spurted out a truth I'd hidden from him for forty years." Jess denies her tears.

"Okay . . . I'm listening. What truth?"

"You may recall that my daughter Rita died from breast cancer last year." Jess's troubled brown eyes nervously vibrate. "Well, I was so mad at John, I told him the truth about Rita."

Lorene's lemony eyes widen. "What truth?"

"John is a twin. Josh looks just like him. Back in college, they often traded places with each other," Jess explains.

"Like attending classes?" Lorene wonders.

"Yes, and other times, too. They are truly identical."

"Oh . . ." Lorene anticipates something unimaginable coming.

"Well, Josh traded places with John the night you girls came over for supper. That's why the subject of Dorothy Powell came up so often. He was trying to pry information out of you. He needs to know where Dorothy is and if she's finished her book."

"Oh." Lorene had read the CIA's account of misdeeds.

"I'm so sorry. I did not know it was Josh until later."

"Wow! This is news I never expected."

"I know, and I'm so, so sorry, Lorene." She swipes a tear from one cheek. "If I knew you girls back then, I wouldn't . . ."

"It's okay, I understand, Jess. Back to the truth you told John that drove you over to my house tonight?" Lorene waits.

"I dated Josh first while in college. Well, the twins traded places often with dates, just for the fun of it," Jess reveals.

"That's awful! I'm sorry, Jess."

"I slept with both John and Josh. By mistake."

"Wow. What a triangle!" Lorene exclaims.

"Yes, but John fell in love with me. I actually loved both—well, until I recognized the malicious behavior Josh exhibits."

This is even better than Dorothy's CIA novel.

"After I married John, Josh came over to see me while John attended a pediatric convention," Jess reveals. "Josh raped me."

"So, you knew the difference that night."

"I did, Lorene. And I fought him, but he forced himself on me." Tears began to fall. "I never told John until tonight."

"And, of course, he was furious at his brother!"

"There's more to it, Lorene. Rita is Josh's daughter."

To that statement, Lorene is mute.

36

JOHN RECEIVED THE phone call from Josh soon after Jessica left the house. He was blown away at the idea that their parents were alive and in Witness Protection in Mexico. John did not tell Josh what Jess told him about Rita. He wanted to confront his naughty twin in person. Even more, he wanted to see his parents.

The flight to Mexico left out of Nashville at midnight. He would fly to Miami, Florida, then board a direct flight to Oaxaca. He'd left a note on the bar for Jess: *Away on business.*

There was a two-hour layover in Miami, so John did not arrive in Oaxaca, Mexico until 11 a.m. Wednesday morning.

No available rental cars, John requested an UBER on his phone and found one. The cost per mile was outrageous, but he had no choice. As he climbed into the backseat of an old Ford sedan, he spied a tall, thin woman exiting a truck.

Hell, if she didn't remind him of Dorothy Powell!

He was losing it. His imagination had gone wild—especially after Jess dropped the filial bomb on him late yesterday.

Does Josh suspect Rita is his biological daughter?

There is no way to know for sure unless John asks him.

Would he lie about raping Jess?

* * *

Dorothy spied the man getting into a Ford sedan ogling her as she climbed down from Diago's junky truck. For a second, she saw recognition in his hazel eyes. But that was impossible. Today, she was wearing Grace Bailey's gray wig and a pair of fake glasses. Her daughter wouldn't recognize her if they met on the street.

Oh, Claire! I have been so unfair to you.

Guilt settles over Dorothy as the terminal's automatic doors open, inviting her into a cooler atmosphere. Yesterday's storm had left the air heavy with humidity and it was blazing hot. No doubt another storm was brewing somewhere close and would erupt.

She only prayed the weather wouldn't delay her flight to Atlanta. She had decided it was unwise to fly directly into Nashville, much safer to travel incognito on a Greyhound bus.

* * *

Jim Grossman had seen no reason to stay in Columbia, Tennessee, searching for Dorothy's notebook since he'd hit a dead-end. If anyone knew anything, they weren't tattling.

So, he'd decided to fly out of Nashville to Mexico and settle his nasty business with his captive. A bullet would do nicely.

As Jim reaches the international gate, people flow into the airport proper and scatter. He waits in line for his turn to board the Delta flight and locates his seat. All he wants to do is sleep. When he confronts Dorothy, he needs to be at his best.

Time falls away until Jim is startled awake by the pilot's voice, announcing the approach to the Oaxaca Airport in Mexico. After a bumpy landing, he grabs his bag from the overhead bin, and quickly deplanes. On his way down the concourse to the exit, he spies an elderly woman wearing a floppy straw hat and dark glasses. As they pass, her large shoulder bag rudely bumps him.

Stupid American on her way home to the states.

It's a long walk to the airport parking lot, so he opts for a bus ride to his Jeep. After tipping the driver, he starts the engine and exits the airport. Mexico's humidity drips off his dirty windshield.

* * *

John Bailey is also in Mexico. As directed by Josh, he leaves his rental car at the edge of a wooded area located at the base of a mountain. He locks up the car, grabs his gear, and begins the trek up the trodden pathway to his parents' cabin. Hard to imagine his conversation with his parents after two years of thinking they were dead. What had his father done to earn a stint with the Witness Protection Program? And why didn't they trust their twin sons?

Is it because Josh is a CIA agent?

Maybe, secrecy was required to keep them safe. John is still learning the depth of deceit the Agency perpetrates.

Nothing good can come from fussing at his parents for their pretense. Evidently, they did what they were told in order to survive. Why Josh had happened upon them at the cabin was a mystery. There were so many facets to any future conversations.

The wooded pathway up the mountain is mushy with rain and John was not wearing the right kind of shoes for the weather. His tennis shoes are quickly soaked as slow rain and humidity play havoc with him. Already mid-afternoon, clouds amassing over the tall trees indicate a thunderstorm is eminent. So, John walks faster up the path, not in as good a shape as he'd like to believe.

Plus, his thoughts are weighty, too.

Finally, the path ends and he enters a clearing, spying a log cabin perilously clinging to the side of a sloping mountain.

As if sensing his approach, Josh is watching him from the front porch. "Hey, bro! You made it!" He calls out.

As John reaches the porch landing, Josh reaches out for him.

"How are Dad and Mom?" John cannot bring himself to hug Josh. He's too angry inside over what Jess had told him.

"They're inside, John!" Josh exclaims. "Come inside and change into some dry clothes. Where's your bag?"

"No bag, I can't stay long. Jess and I had a big fight."

Josh rocks his head. "Women. You can't trust them and you can't live without them! What 're we gonna do, Bro?"

"John!" Grace nearly collapses on her younger son. Josh had been born three minutes before his brother. She hadn't known she was pregnant with twins until she gave birth. The preemies had stayed in the hospital prenatal room for nearly two months.

"Mom! Thank God you're alive!" John hails as he sees his father standing behind Grace. "Dad!" They hug tightly.

Grace says, "You're a sweaty mess, son. Josh, show John to the bathroom and get him a change of clothes."

"I didn't take the time to pack, Mama."

"It's okay, son. Your father's clothes will fit okay."

Josh walks John down the hall to the bathroom. He removes a towel from the hall closet and hands it to his brother.

"What did you and Jess fight about?" Josh asks.

"Not now, I'm too tired. We'll talk about it later."

"Okay." Josh squints his eyes.

Is this about his ruse with Jess the night of the cookout?

John shivers, suddenly cold.

"I'll get you some clothes while you shower and shave."

"Thanks." John shuts the door and leans against it.

Is it possible Jess lied to me about Josh?

37

DOROTHY RODE THE Greyhound Bus from Atlanta to Nashville and phoned Claire to come get her. She'd sat on a bench outside the terminal for over thirty minutes waiting for her daughter.

She recognizes Claire's Buick and hurriedly approaches.

"Get in, Mama!" Claire hails from the driver's seat, the car idling. "You have a lot of explaining to do."

"Good to see you, too, daughter!" She walks around the back of the Buick and gets in the passenger seat. "How are you?"

"About to be divorced from Theodore," Claire says as she pulls out into the Nashville traffic. "How is Tom?"

"I don't know, I haven't seen him since last Friday."

Claire takes the I-40 into Nashville and adjusts the GPS for HOME. For the past twenty minutes, neither have said a word.

"When is the divorce final, Claire?"

She chuckles. "And here I thought you'd ask me why we were getting a divorce, Mama." Claire looks perturbed.

"I don't need to ask a question I already know the answer to, Claire. Ted cheated on you, had a son, and now he wants nothing to do with you. Get over your heartaches, and move on."

"Wow!" Claire is shocked. "What happened to motherly love?" This reunion is nothing like she'd expected.

Dorothy sighs. "It's not like I'm not sympathetic with your feelings, dear. It's just that sympathy, even empathy, is not worth the words written on a page. They accomplish nothing."

"Okay . . . you sound like the voice of experience."

"I am!" She looks hard a Claire. "No matter how hard I try to do the right things, bad circumstances always chase me down."

"Don't tell me yet, Mama. Let's get home and have some coffee. This appears to be a long conversation I really don't want to start while I am driving." She increases her speed.

"I knew I raised a smart daughter!"

***

Back in Mexico, Jim Grossman arrives at the Bailey's cabin after sunset. The UBER driver got lost since the address wasn't on the GPS system. But he had a print map showing the main roads.

The walk up the incline had been difficult in the dark, even with his high-powered flashlight. When the woods fell away and he spied the cabin on the hill, it almost felt like home.

Jim doesn't knock on the door. It isn't locked.

Inside, he hears voices from the kitchen. Four voices.

"Well, look who the cat's dragged up!" Jim exclaims from the doorway, his weapon drawn and ready to fire at John Bailey.

"You!" John recognizes his visitor at his home. Josh's friend, my eye! Don't shoot, Jim. I'm not here to cause trouble."

"Where is Dorothy Powell?" Jim looks at Gerald Bailey.

Grace rises from the dining table and answers, "You're too late, she's gone. We tried to keep her here, but couldn't."

Jim knows it's a lie, but he won't provoke his hostess.

"How did you find your parents?" Jim asks John.

The younger twin looks at Josh to answer the question the CIA agent with the gun asked. It's not his mess to clean up.

"Well, hello, James." Josh stands and pushes away from the table. "The CIA's favorite assassin who would kill his mother for a reward." He glances over at his mother. "We'll be fine."

Grace is shivering. She didn't feel fine.

Jim's lips wiggle, not actually a smile, more like amusement.

"Thanks for the compliment, Josh." He motions with his .44 revolver for everyone to sit down. "So, Gerald, about Dorothy?"

Gerald shakes his head. "Wasn't my idea, Jim. I keep my promises. The girls pulled one over on me. All we know is she's gone, not where she is." He squeezes Grace's hand.

"Well . . . seems we have a problem." Jim locks cold eyes on Josh. "How did you know to come here?"

"I spoke to Director Carlton. He told me where to look."

"I find that intriguing." Jim chuckles. "He told me you didn't have the guts to permanently solve the Dorothy problem, so he sent a *man* for the job." He sobers. "*The* man with the gun."

"Looks like you failed miserably," John chimes in.

"He speaks his mind. The twin who heals babies for a job instead of saving America from its enemies." Jim's narrow gaze slides to Grace. "How did you birth two boys so different?"

"I'm not responsible, Agent Grossman. That's God's job."

"Well, if you think God is going to save them now, you've got the whole universe thing wrong. I'm in charge, Mama."

* * *

Claire and her mother are seated at the breakfast bar on stools drinking coffee and catching up on the past week's events when Helen walks through the backdoor with her two children.

"GG!" June runs to Dorothy and hugs her legs. "Did the buggerman steal you from us? I'm so glad you beat him up.!"

"Grammy, thank God you're safe." Helen hugs Dorothy.

"Of course, I'm safe, ye of little faith." Dorothy looks down at her grandson. "How are you, Billy? Playing a lot of baseball?"

He nods and climbs in his GG's lap.

"We've all been so worried about you," Helen utters. "Mama even had a memorial service for you at Ellie's farm. Brother Kenny conducted the service. But Lorene Perkins never believed you were dead, However, everyone else there bought the lie."

"We went up high in a balloon, GG," June utters. "We tossed the ashes on the cow pasture. You should've seen them blow."

"I bet." Dorothy laughs. "You can thank Tom for the ashes. It was his idea to send the urn. But first, he had to convince a mortician in Belize to donate the remains for a good cause."

"It was a beautiful memorial service, Grammy, I even cried." Helen sniffles. "Don't ever scare us like that again."

"I'm still not safe," Dorothy tells Claire. "But I won't go easy, that's for sure. I still have to get my book published."

"About your notes in the guest bedroom," Claire says, "I thought someone had broken in the house and stolen them."

"I needed a safer place for them, Claire. Lorene Perkins had a key to your house and took them while you were a church."

"I know. She told me," Claire says.

"She also has my completed book."

"What book?" June asks, always curious about everything.

"I wrote about some bad guys who hurt me, honey. I hope when people read it, they will make those awful people pay."

"How much money?" June asks.

Helen explains, "Grammy is talking about putting those bad people in prison for the trouble they've caused her."

June looks at Dorothy. "What trouble, GG?"

"Let's just say it will all work for good and leave it at that," Claire chimes in. The kids are too young to understand.

"Mama, can you keep the kids over the weekend?"

"What's going on, Helen?"

"Patrick and I are taking a trip. We need some alone time."

"Sure." Claire looks at her mother. "Will you be staying the weekend with us, too?"

"Pretty please, GG! We can pop corn and watch movies."

"Another time, June. I need to explain my situation to the girls in Columbia," Dorothy explains. "But I will stay tonight."

"Good!" Claire has a lot more questions about where her wayward mother has been and what she was doing with Tom.

"Thanks, Mama," Helen says. "I need to get on home and pack our bags for the weekend. Thanks for helping out."

Claire hops off the barstool. "No problem, dear."

"Give GG a big hug, June. You, too, Billy," Helen says.

Dorothy wraps her arms around her two great-grandchildren, breathing a prayer for their safety and a good life forward.

After Helen and the kids had gone, Dorothy explains to Claire why she'd left Columbia so abruptly last November. Tom had warned her the CIA was on the warpath again. He'd sent her a ticket to Belize in Central America, then switched her ticket to Mexico, where he'd met her at the airport. They'd driven to Belize and moved into a tree house in the jungle. They were happy and felt safe for six months, until the CIA found them.

"One agent wanted to capture me. One wanted me dead."

"So that's why you sent the ashes," Claire concludes.

"Yes. Tom thought if the CIA believed I was dead, they'd stop looking. Turns out he was wrong. The Agency is relentless, but they've never faced a more determined woman than me."

"Mama, you're scaring me."

"You told June good would win out. It will, Claire."

"How in the world did you escape both agents?"

"With help from a good woman," Dorothy explains. "I was left in the care of an elderly couple, Gerald and Grace Bailey."

"Bailey? I know that name, Mama." She holds up a finger in thought. "John and Jessica Bailey came to your memorial service."

"Is it possible they are related?" It's a small world, after all.

"Maybe. Jess is a friend of Lorene's, and has been playing Canasta in your place while you've been away," Claire explains.

"Have you spoken to Lorene about my book?"

"No, but you said you'd finished it. When?"

"Soon after I left the states with Tom," Dorothy replies.

"Where is it?"

"In a safe place, honey. Best you don't know."

"I see. Well, you can't trust Tom, Mama. He's CIA through and through. Most of what he's done is cause you trouble."

"He loves me, Claire. I don't doubt that."

"Then, where is he now when you need him?"

"I don't know, dear. We got separated Friday a week ago in Belize," Dorothy explains. "Agent Jim Grossman kidnapped me."

"Do you think he killed Tom?"

"He wasn't dead when we drove away. Jim slashed his tires, so he wasn't able to follow us. But I know he's still looking."

"So, Jim took you to a cabin in Mexico?"

"Yes. After Grace gave me one of her wigs and her passport, I left early on Tuesday and found a cabin higher up the mountain. A young couple took me in for the night. Maria's husband Diago drove me to the airport on Wednesday. I flew to Atlanta, and rode a Greyhound bus to Nashville. The rest you know."

Dorothy pauses.

"What are you going to do now, Mama?"

"Finish what I started.

Claire shakes her head.

"What, dear?"

"This nightmare never seems to end."

38

"PUT THE GUN DOWN," Gerald Bailey tells Jim Grossman. "We are not going to fight you. You're making my wife nervous."

"Dad's right," Josh agrees. "We can work out this problem without violence. We want the same thing. To find Dorothy."

"What about you, John? Are you on board?"

"I'm not an agent. I don't know how to use a gun."

Jim lowers his weapon and approaches the table. Gerald gets a straight chair from a closet for him to sit. "Okay, let's talk."

"By now, Dorothy is back in Tennessee," Gerald says.

"I wish you hadn't told him that," Grace protests.

"Where do you think she'll go?" Jim asks John, aware he resides in Columbia. "Does your wife know you're here?"

"Actually, that's none of your business!" John exclaims.

"Careful, son," Gerald warns, sensing Jim is trigger-happy.

"She's best friends with Lorene Perkins. Two other women also play in Dorothy's Canasta Club on Fridays," he reveals.

"Have you been spying on her, John??" Jim asks.

"Josh asked me to keep my eyes open," he replies.

Jim says, "I've searched Lorene's house and found nothing useful. No notebook or completed book Dorothy has written."

"You doubt she has the ability to do it?" Grace asks.

"I doubt she has the courage!" Jim snarls.

"She does!" Thomas Kessler appears in the doorway, a pointed automatic Glock in his right hand. "Hello, Jim!"

The CIA assassin rears back and laughs. "Well, well, the gang is all here. This is getting more interesting by the minute."

"What's so funny?" Grace asks Jim.

"All of us here. Except Dorothy," he answers.

"Where is she?" Tom asks Jim, wavering the gun.

"She went home to Columbia," Grace answers.

"Honey, let me handle this," Gerald tells her.

"It's been a while since we talked, Tom."

"Not long enough," Tom says to Jim. "I haven't missed you at all. In fact, my life has been rather peaceful."

"Well, I'd say that phase of romance has ended."

Grace gets up from the table. "Well, guys, I'm going to let you battle it out while I make us some supper. Whoever is left standing is welcome to eat at my table." She looks at the guys.

"Put the gun away, Tom. We're just negotiating," Josh says.

"I don't trust this bully, so why should I?"

John says, "He's agreed to peacefully resolve our Dorothy problem. You know her best, so let's get to it."

* * *

Claire's guest bed was comfortable, but Dorothy could not sleep, so she packed the few clothes that Grace gave her, then called an UBER. This time she left a note on the bar for Claire stating she was going to see Lorene Perkins.

The trip to Maury County takes forty-five minutes. Dorothy gives the Uber driver a tip and exits the car, grateful she still has Tom's credit card hidden under the sole of one white sandal.

Men are no match for clever women.

Lorene opens the door at 2 a.m. Friday morning and takes a wild look at Dorothy, then slams the door in her face.

She knocks again. Harder, this time.

The door comes open. Lorene glares through bleary eyes.

"Is it really you, Dorothy, or am I having a bad dream?"

She snickers, and pushes open the door. "First time I've been called a bad dream. But yes, it's me, friend. We need to talk."

Lorene slumps into the kitchen and shakes the coffee pot to see if there's any left over from yesterday. Then looks at Dorothy.

"Do I need to perk coffee? Maybe we should both sleep first." Lorene sets the empty pot on the bar. "You say."

"Perk the Double D-D coffee, Lorene, we need to talk."

Fifteen minutes later, they are seated in the den. The knot lodged in Dorothy's dry throat comes unglued and spews words like snake venom at Agent James Grossman, the assassin who had kidnapped her. There's so much to tell she doesn't know where to stop. As Lorene listens, her eyes reflect shock at the impossible story. Dorothy stops and looks at her. "Well, aren't you going to say something?" She bug-eyes Lorene. "Like, I'm so sorry."

"Why didn't he kill you?"

Dorothy lets loose a belabored sigh. "I suppose if Jim had, it would solve a lot of people's problems. Tom could find another girl who looks like his first wife, fall in love, and torment her. And Jim Grossman could move on with his assassination career."

Lorene holds up a hand. "I'm glad he didn't, Dorothy, but it doesn't make sense that he stashed you in a cabin and left Mexico. Where did he go for—how many days was he gone?"

"Lorene, that sentence doesn't make sense."

"Exactly my point. The guy kidnaps you, says he's going to kill you. Could have shot you then and there. And leaves."

Acknowledgment dawns in Dorothy's expression.

"Did I just answer your question?"

"You sure did, Lorene. Jim wants both my notebook and book destroyed. He has to make sure it doesn't reach the light of day. Destroying me won't guarantee the book isn't published."

"I don't know, Dorothy, the CIA has their ways."

"That's why I have a new plan."

"You don't want the book published?" Lorene tries to track Dorothy's tricky mind all over the place and still scattering.

"Here's what I want you to do . . ."

* * *

The negotiation between Jim, Josh, John, and Tom lasted hours until they were too weary to talk. Too much food had been consumed and they were sleepy. Gerald and Grace Bailey had already gone to bed. And it was storming outdoors again.

"Does it ever stop dropping liquid?" Jim groans.

"Rain is complimentary in Mexico," Josh jokes.

Tom remarks, "Here's how we are going to play it, guys. Like I told Jack Carlton, I will make sure Dorothy doesn't publish her book. In fact, I will see to it personally that nothing is left for her to print. Okay? And you should know, I'm going to marry her."

"Why?" Jim asks. "She's a handful."

Josh laughs. "An interesting old woman, ask me."

"And smart as an astronaut. She's stayed light years ahead of us and received no CIA training. Give Dorothy some credit."

"Okay, I won't shoot her the next time I see her," Jim says.

"I'm going home to water my plants. I know they're half dead by now," Josh says. "The American south is having a drought."

"So now, can we all get some sleep? Later today, I'm off to Columbia to confront Dorothy about the book," Tom says.

Josh looks at John, who has been observant though silent through the negotiation. "We need to talk, Bro."

"I agree." John motions for Josh to step out on the covered back porch. A swift wind hits him as he opens the kitchen door.

"I need to apologize to you, John."

"For what?" For a second, John wonders if his twin brother has read his mind. He's prepared to tell him about Rita.

"Scaring Jess when we traded places at your house."

"Oh, that . . . she'll get over it."

"No, you have a great marriage, Bro. I'm envious, and I would do nothing to jeopardize your relationship with Jess. She's been a great mother to Rita. And no father could be better."

"You are right, Josh, no father could do better." He stares into the inky rainy night. "Family means everything."

"Earlier, you said you had something we needed to talk about. What's bothering you?" Josh stares at his scruffy boots.

"Just that I appreciate your calling me about Dad and Mom. You might have kept it a secret, but you didn't. I want to speak to the people in charge of the Witness Protection Program and see if I can bring them home. We can both watch after them."

"Columbia or Atlanta?"

"Let them decide," John answers.

"How do you intend to protect them from the Mafia?" Josh asks. "The Russians have eyes all over the world."

"Dad and Mom can keep their assumed names and creds. As long as we both keep our mouths shut, they should be fine."

"Okay, I should be the one to talk to the Director."

"Thanks, Bro," John says, resigned that he'd made the right decision by not telling Josh that Rita was his biological daughter.

39

JESSICA BAILEY IS restless in her big king-size bed. John has been missing since late Tuesday. They argued over Joshua then she left the house. When she got home late, he was gone. She'd called a few of his friends in Atlanta, but they hadn't heard from him.

He was livid when she walked out of the house three days ago. It is already Friday morning and not a word from him.

Jess glances at the bedside clock. *3:45 a.m.*

Puttering into the bathroom, she retrieves a Benadryl and a Tylenol, pops them in her mouth then washes the meds down with a glass of water. Too early to start her busy day.

I have to be at the Senior Citizen Center by lunch.

Jess questions if Lorene Perkins kept her secret about her daughter Rita's birth father. When John got over his anger, would they resolve things? Or would he ask for a divorce?

I should have trusted him with my secret.

* * *

Two o'clock rolls around on Friday and the girls are seated at the round table on the back patio of the Senior Citizen Center. Lorene has dealt the first Canasta hand when a shadow falls over her. She looks up. "Dorothy! I wondered if you'd show."

"You knew she was back in town!" Lizzy exclaims.

"I told her not to tell anyone," Dorothy says. "Hi, Jessica. I'm Dorothy Powell, the troublemaker. Thanks for taking my place."

Feeling awkward, Jess rises from her seat. "Here."

"No, keep your seat, I'll watch." Dorothy pulls up a chair and sits beside Lorene. "I'd rather rest, if that's okay."

Jane says, "I'm so glad you aren't dead, Dorothy."

"Me, too." Dorothy looks at Jess. "I heard your husband was out of town—Lorene told me. Is he back yet?"

Jess shakes her head no, uncomfortable with elaborating.

"Well, I'm expecting the recovery crew to show up any moment," Dorothy says. "You girls need to be prepared."

"Prepared how?" Lizzy lays her cards down on the table.

"I suppose you've noticed I'm the star of the CIA show." Lizzy snickers.

"Is she always this much fun?" Jess asks.

"You have no idea." Jane smiles.

"I can't think straight enough to play cards today," Lorene says. "Why don't we all go somewhere private and talk? If we work together, I'm sure we can find a way to save Dorothy."

"Who said I need saving?" Dorothy sputters. "I can watch my own six." She'd picked up Tom's CIA lingo.

"Count me out, girls." Jess turns up her cards. "By the way, I had four red threes." She grins at Lorene. "Give me 800 points."

"Good to meet you, Jess," Dorothy says as the pretty blond grabs her lizard-skin purse off the floor and walks away.

"What's her problem?" Dorothy asks Lorene.

"It's not you, dear. She has husband problems."

"Okay, I won't ask," Dorothy says.

"I will," Jane hails. "What are you not saying Lorene."

"I'm keeping Jess's secret, that's all."

"Since when?" Lizzy chimes in. "There are no secrets in Columbia. Check the Grapevine."

Dorothy laughs. "Not much has changed since I went away," she comments. "I can't say that doesn't please me."

They end up at Lizzy's house. Lorene had pointed out that if the CIA assassin returned to Columbia looking for Dorothy, the first place he'd come was her house. Jane and Dorothy agreed.

It was a lengthy discussion. Dorothy started at the beginning when Tom had phoned her and asked to meet her for coffee. She'd learned that the CIA had put out a contract on her life.

"So, you ran," Jane says.

"Tom and I hid out in Belize until Agent James Grossman tracked us down. He slashed Tom's car tires and kidnapped me."

"Why didn't he just shoot you then and there?" Lizzy asks.

"He had to make sure the book didn't get published."

"Where is your infamous notebook and manuscript?" Jane inquires. "Did you send it to a publisher?"

"Working on it." Dorothy winks at Lorene.

* * *

When Dorothy returns with Lorene to her house, there is a rental car parked in the driveway.

"Tom or Jim?" Lorene wonders.

"Let's go see." Dorothy opens the front door.

"I'm sure I locked it," Lorene says. "I know I did."

"And I'm sure whoever is inside didn't care a whit!"

They walked through the foyer. Tom was in the kitchen devouring a slice of chess pie. "Hi, darling," he calls out to Dorothy, gazing wickedly at her. "We've missed you."

"Who's we?" Lorene asks.

"Jim Grossman said to give you his regards."

"You found him?" Dorothy feels behind on the script.

"Don't worry, he's not going to kill you."

"Why not?" Lorene inquires.

"Let's just say we came to an agreement."

"That's good for Dorothy, but who gave you permission to break into my house?" Lorene stares at her burglar.

"I found the extra key under the back porch floormat."

"Oh . . ." Lorene shrugs. "That."

"Details matter," says Dorothy, swooning over Tom. She's so in love it's making her sick. How did she become so foolish?

"Lorene, can I talk to Dorothy alone?"

"Be my guest. On the back porch."

Dorothy walks out the door first, feeling Tom's light touch on her back. She wants to turn around and plant a sloppy kiss on his moist lips, but she should not make it so easy for him. He'll get the upper hand and she'd never get it back. They sit in the swing.

Nearly dark, mosquitoes buzz around in the backyard.

"Aren't you going to ask where Jim took me?"

"I know where you've been, Dorothy. I spent a couple of day with Gerald and Grace Bailey at their mountain cabin in Mexico."

"I see."

"Nice place, if you enjoy prison," Tom says.

"Grace helped me escape Jim's murderous clutches."

"She told me. Seemed proud of your bravery."

Dorothy gives him a sideward glance. "Why didn't Jim shoot you?" She sits back in the swing, inhaling his enticing cologne.

That Romeo son-of-a-gun!

"You look beautiful tonight, Dorothy."

She shrugs. "You're a no-good, dirty-plotting CIA agent, Thomas Kessler. How can I trust anything you tell me?"

His kiss pretty much solidified that answer.

"Here's how it's going to work, Dorothy. You are not going to publish your damn book! And you are going to marry me!"

"Done."

"Which one?"

"What you said," she replies. "When's the wedding?"

"Well, we're sure not putting it off, honey. Why not this Sunday. It gives you all day Saturday to plan. I already have the license to make it legal. Applied at the Columbia Courthouse earlier today. We can have a small quiet wedding."

"I don't want a small, quiet wedding, Tom! I want all my friends to watch me commit harry-carry with the guy I can't trust. If you ever decide to off me, God help you!"

Tom snickers. "Okay. No book, then?"

"You can destroy all the copies."

Tom twists his lips to one side. "Why does this feel so easy? I expected a fight, and you give me no resistance?"

"Isn't that what you want?"

"Something feels off."

"Don't you trust me, honey?'

"Not a far as I can throw you."

* * *

John was home by the time Jess arrived around 3 p.m. Friday. "Where have you been?" was her first question.

"To Mexico. My parents are alive."

"What?" Jess can't believe her ears. "How did you find out?"

"Josh phoned right after you left the house on Tuesday."

"Did you tell him about Rita?" she asks.

"No, he convinced me not to."

"How did he do that?" She sits down on the sofa.

From the recliner, he answers, "Josh told me he was sorry he scared you the night he traded places with me—the Friday night when your Canasta friends came over for a cookout," John explains. "He also said you were a great mother to Rita, and I had done a better job as a dad raising her than he ever could."

"Do you think he realizes Rita was his daughter?" Jess asks.

"He never said. And I didn't tell him. I guess some things are best left unsaid when it comes to family, Jess. I don't want to alienate him from our lives. And we agreed to bring our parents home to America. He's going to speak to the CIA Director."

"Then all is well that ends well," Jess says. "Am I forgiven?"

"If you'll forgive me for putting my brother's wishes in front of yours so many times, Jess. I want to move back to Atlanta."

"Dorothy Powell is back in town."

"I suspected that. What do you want to do about moving? Dad and Mom want to live in Atlanta and I need to keep a close watch on them. They will keep their assumed names."

"They were in Witness Protection?"

"Yes, but they are approaching their nineties. They should not be punished for something they accidentally witnessed."

"I agree," Jess says. "Okay, I'll phone a Realtor on Monday and arrange for the packers to come. We'll do it quickly."

"Thank you, Jess."

"You can do better than that." She leads her husband into the bedroom. "This bed has been crying out for you since Tuesday."

40

SUNDAY MORNING CAME bright and early with low humidity and gentle breezes suffusing the city of Columbia, Tennessee. All is well with its citizens. Somehow, God has blessed all those who are troubled and have rectified difficult circumstances.

Dorothy is waiting in the wing of the church where the choir usually enters the church sanctuary for services. She is wearing an ankle-length pink lace dress and a silver tiara with a thin white veil over her face. Hopefully, it will hide any new wrinkles since she's marrying a man almost young enough to be her son.

Well, I've actually done more foolish things.

The organist is playing the prelude to the Wedding March. More anxious than when she first wed, Dorothy thoughts leap back to the day Arthur Powell waited for her to walk the aisle.

She snickers. They were young and so in love.

For decades, life went exactly as they'd planned. Two children, a girl and a boy. A farm setting. A truly good life.

Until one day it wasn't.

It all began the day Arthur and Crawford Perkins became privy to information that upset the Russian Mafia. The guys knew they were in danger and planned for their deaths. Both purchased life insurance policies, naming their wives as the recipients.

But that is all water under the bridge now . . .

She is not young anymore, but opportunity has once more offered her a chance at happiness. Thomas Kessler is not always honest with her, but there's no doubt he loves her.

He will fight for me no matter the obstacle.

She loves him for that. So, she'd sacrificed her original copy of the book the CIA hated, then watched him burn its precious pages that took years to write. Next her notebook went into the fireplace flames. It felt like she'd lost a child. Yet, cleansing.

Tom had not asked her if she'd made a copy, and only a fool would have volunteered that information. It was a secret only for a best friend. Dorothy can't help smile at her witty plan.

The CIA Director had been satisfied that she was no longer a threat to the Agency. And Tom was officially retiring from the CIA and moving to Columbia. Regrettably, he'd returned the million dollars he stolen from Uncle Sam, but was rewarded for solving their problem. They no longer wanted to kill his bride.

They believe I am no threat.

There's a huge difference, Dorothy still has a few tricks up her sleeve. Keeping your mouth shut is the key to success.

And I am really good at keeping secrets.

John and Jessica Bailey's beautiful home on the Columbia Golf Course came up for sale and Tom had put in a contract for purchase. Dorothy cannot imagine what it will feel like to be upper-class. She might even have to join the Garden Club.

She hears the Wedding March.

Time to shine.

Claire is her Matron of Honor and her great-grandchildren are the flower bunnies. Little Billy refused to be a Flower Girl.

The idea makes Dorothy laugh.

Go ahead, girl. This is your day!

Tom stands with Joshua Bailey to the left of Brother Kenny, her devoted Methodist pastor. The stage is decorated with flaming candles and dozens of red roses mingled with lacy fern greenery. All she has to do is pay attention and say "I do."

Deader 'n a Doornail

SIX MONTHS LATER

TOM READ IN THE Nashville *Tennessean* where Jackson Carlton had stepped down as CIA Director. The entire organization was undergoing a radical regime change, ordered by the President of the United States. It appeared certain critical information had come forward that indicated the CIA had improperly stolen American funds in the early 1990s, and placed them in foreign banks. Tom lowers paper and looks hard at Dorothy.

"What?" she asks, a cup of Joe in one hand.
"What did you do, Dorothy?"
"What do you think I did, Tom?"
"The CIA Director has been fired."
"Well, hallelujah! God pulled one over on them!"
Tom isn't smiling.
"Dorothy . . ."
"I know. But you know I love you."
He cannot help but grin.
Oh, boy! Here we go again!

About the Author

M. Sue Alexander has written over forty novels. Many are published on Amazon Books for e-book download or paperback purchases. In 1958, she graduated high school in Bolivar, Tennessee, and earned a Bachelor of Science Degree from Union University in Jackson, Tennessee in 1962. For decades she devoted her attention to writing and recording original songs while working first as a public-school teacher during the 1970s before becoming licensed to sell residential real estate in three states. In 2003, she began publishing her books online. The 12-book *Resurrection Dawn 2014* series is based on End Times biblical prophecy. *Time of Jacob's Trouble* continues the saga as Christians face challenges in a world hostile to the Gospel message. Her *Crystal Creek Mystery* series was inspired during a Canasta game. Protagonist Dorothy Powell is the epitome of hope for elderly readers seeking a more exciting life. This series is both funny and serious, sometimes preposterous, and deals with the mental, emotional, and physical hoops older women must leap through to achieve happiness. View her books online.

Martha Alexander's SPYTRAP

Enter the world of mystery and intrigue where good versus evil thrives in secret places. The impulses, actions, and words of the story characters on opposing sides reveal their deepest desires to find their place in society where they best fit and can achieve success. That includes prestige and wealth. ATF (Alcohol, Tobacco, and Firearms) Agent Lincoln Barry works diligently to fight crime in America alongside other devoted agents during the 1970s. Young and ambitious, he's married and has a young daughter. Keeping his family safe and far removed from his sordid work world is a priority, but someone has put a target on Linc's back. A spy trap has been set as payback for messing with the New Orleans Dixie Mafia. Agent Barry's assignments take him into the darkest corners of life where degenerates live and occasionally thrive. He soon realizes he's not all that different from the people he tricks and arrests. Over time, he's become addicted to violence and the thrill of the chase. Linc's trauma sometimes spills over into his family life. Based on the true cases of a retired federal agent, this compelling story is both entertaining and informative. Enjoy *Spytrap*.

Coming 2025: BLOODTRAP! Based on the true case assignments carried out by a retired ATF agent. Don't miss reading this spy-thriller!